Launch into Love

KIRSTEN BAILEY

Copyright © 2024 Kirsten Bailey

All rights reserved.

ISBN: 9798304193122

CHAPTERS

1	1
2	5
3	14
4	18
5	24
6	30
7	32
8	34
9	39
10	42
11	48
12	50
13	57
14	61
15	65
16	73
17	78
18	81
19	93
20	95
21	97
22	101
23	108
24	111
25	112
26	115
27	117
28	119
29	122
30	124
31	127
32	132
33	134
34	136
MORE BY KIRSTEN BAILEY	139

1
Emily

Emily stood by the kitchen window and watched as an unfamiliar blue van pulled up on the road. It looked old and dented, with a crooked front bumper. Despite its shabby appearance, someone had made half-hearted attempts to repair it, securing loose parts of the chassis with fabric tape. The vehicle reminded Emily of her mother's cakes. Around holidays like Christmas or Easter and before birthdays, her mother would feel compelled to bake something special. However, these attempts often failed. The cakes would either burn or fall apart due to missing ingredients like eggs. As a result, her mother would pour vanilla icing over the top, trying to decorate the disaster with sprinkles.

On the left side of the van, a new bright red sliding door had been installed. The van seemed to say, "Hey, I've been in a few accidents and might break down soon, but my owner still believes in me enough to invest in spare parts. Come on, get in, at least I'm still running!"

Drivers who took Emily and her classmates to school typically used their cars, as the students were scattered over a wide area, making it unprofitable to employ buses. For a while, Emily had ridden with the junior manager of a funeral home. After dropping the students off, the manager would remove the back rows of seats, install a partition, and spend the rest of the morning transporting corpses. Despite the unusual circumstances, Emily had liked this driver because of her smooth driving style. Having experienced some near-death situations, Emily was prepared for anything. Her school backpack contained travel sickness pills, a bottle of vanilla-scented oil (a necessity in this area when the wind blew in from the pork farms), and business cards for her YouTube channel, hoping to one day connect with an adult who could discuss something other than bad weather, highway roadworks, or soccer.

Impatiently, the driver honked the horn.

"I'm coming!" Emily called out.

She dashed down the garden path and climbed over a plywood frame. Her mother had been working outside late into the night, leaving everything in disarray. Most likely, she was busy planning her next cabaret festival or some other event. Since Emily wasn't speaking to her at the moment, she had no way of knowing. She headed for the passenger door. Being the first one on the route was fortunate because it meant she could take the front seat, where she would be least likely to feel nauseous. With a shudder, she recalled a student from the previous year who had just earned his driver's license and still struggled to shift gears, making his old Volvo bounce around.

"Good morning!" Emily called out cheerfully.

Being friendly was essential. If you upset the driver, you could easily be "forgotten" at school during lunchtime and left to find your way home alone. With a mother who often disappeared into her studio for hours and didn't respond to her phone, that meant sitting on the gym steps, doing homework with a grumbling stomach, until mother emerged from her artistic fever for a bathroom break and realized Emily was missing. The driver (who Emily guessed was a woman because of her pink lipstick) beckoned her to come in. She wore a green swimming cap.

"Let's go," the driver called.

Emily approached the vehicle.

"Just a moment," she replied.

She turned back towards the house. All the windows were dark. If she woke her mother, she'd likely be in a bad mood, complaining that she couldn't find inspiration now because she was lacking sleep. Additionally, it was uncertain whether Emily's mother would remember the message from school about the new driver; for her, such matters fell into the "unimportant details" category, along with things like transferring money for the school trip, buying milk, and scheduling the annual appointment with the chimney sweep. Pulling her phone from her backpack, Emily dialed the secretary's office. No one picked up. It was just after seven o'clock, and the secretary typically didn't arrive until 7:30 a.m. Emily couldn't afford to wait that long. Classes started at 7:45, and the drive would take half an hour.

Peering through the back windows, Emily noticed that the van had two benches arranged at right angles to the direction of travel, with fitted cupboards above and a small kitchen unit complete with a mini sink and hotplate behind the driver's seat. It appeared to have been upgraded to a camper, which would be handy if they broke down, as they could prepare a meal while waiting for a tow truck.

But did Emily want to break down with this woman? Aside from the swimming cap, the driver looked ordinary. She was wearing a fleece jacket and jeans. Mind you, Emily would also try to look harmless if she were nuts. Before going out, she would dress inconspicuously, practice relaxation exercises in front of the mirror until the crazed grin faded, and then she would venture out to collect unsuspecting young girls. However, while attempting to appear normal, she might overlook one important detail: she was still wearing swimming gear.

At the back of the bus were two moving boxes, but a sports bag was nowhere to be seen. What was Emily supposed to do? She really wanted to believe that there was a logical explanation for the swimming cap.

"My name is Paula," the woman said.

She looked young, not yet thirty, though Emily thought that impression might be due to the tight-fitting cap smoothing out her wrinkles.

"Will you get in?" Paula asked.

Her eyes were heavily made up, with mascara and eyeshadow that matched the color of the swimming cap. The look reminded Emily of an alien. After having ridden in a hearse, various small animal transporters, and a discarded fire engine, nothing should shock her anymore. But this creature in her spaceship frightened her.

2

Jonathan

Jonathan was four glasses into a bottle of cheap red wine when he got the call. He used to think it was a cliché to be unemployed and drink in the afternoon, but now that he was in this situation, he numbed his mind to get through the long hours. He did the shopping and cooking every morning, but still didn't have anything else to fill his time. Anyway, it didn't matter; no one cared what Jonathan did.

Undecided, he looked down at the phone. The display showed the Munich area code, and for a brief, hopeful moment Jonathan thought that Mrs Kaiser might be calling to ask him to work with her daughter again. But when he picked up the phone and heard sobbing, his hope evaporated like a drop of blood in a fifty-metre pool. It was only his former protégé on the line, and unfortunately the young Kaiser had no authority over her sporting future.

"I'm going to kill myself!" Viv wailed.

"No, don't," Jonathan said weakly. As he spoke he realised how heavy his tongue felt. The fact that he hadn't noticed it before, because he hadn't spoken to anyone during his day of drinking, depressed him even more.

"My time in the hundred metre breaststroke has gone up another second," Viv said. "That means I won't even qualify for the nationals."

"There's always next year," Jonathan replied.

"I'm sure I won't make it then either. I'm getting worse under the new coach. Mum says I have to improve by at least a tenth of a second every month.

Those were my words, Jonathan thought grimly.

"You're only 14," he said. "Hormones tend to go crazy at your age."

"But what if I never make it to the top? It'll all be for nothing. I'll have nothing to show for it."

"Well, well," Jonathan murmured.

But Jonathan thought Viv was right. Her life revolved around training, school, homework and then more training. She went to bed early in the evenings to recover and get in shape for training in the morning. He understood how much Viv sacrificed for her sport; after all, he had been her coach for three years - until that unfortunate Wednesday. He remembered them practising breaststroke together. Viv would always stretch her arms out too early to glide for the last few metres. She had one more stroke in her.

On that unfortunate day he had paced along the pool and shouted at Viv: "Leg work! Make sure you use your thighs!"

When Viv finally complied, he clapped his hands and did a spin. Just then he noticed two people sitting on plastic chairs in front of the window at the entrance to the pool. One of them was Viv's mother, Mrs Kaiser. If she didn't have any important appointments, she would pick Viv up from her afternoon training. However, she usually didn't arrive more than twenty minutes early. This should have made Jonathan suspicious, but he was distracted by the second figure - a heavyset man in a bright blue suit, about Jonathan's age, in his early thirties. Jonathan recognised the man but couldn't remember his name.

"Take the kickboard and swim 200 metres using your legs," Jonathan instructed Viv. "Make sure you keep the tension in your lower back."

The man in blue waved. Jonathan pointed to his shoes and mimed rolling up his trouser legs. If the man wanted something, he should come in.

If you searched for Jonathan online, you would find a website that said:

Jonathan Menke
*1987
European runner-up 2008
Coach

You can find me at the Ramstein Aquatic Centre:
Monday to Friday: 6:30am - 8:00am (triathlon training) and 3:00pm - 6:00pm (group and individual training for children and teenagers).

There was no postal address, email contact or phone number. Anyone wishing to contact Jonathan had to visit him at the pool. This not only saved him time, but also tested how interested people were in talking to him. Once, an insurance agent had set up camp on a deck chair and presented Jonathan with the latest policy options. Jonathan decided to take out a policy with her. He felt that commitment deserved to be rewarded.

Ambitious parents of promising young athletes found themselves in a similar position. While waiting for Jonathan to finish coaching his athletes, they learnt an important lesson in patience and got a taste of what to expect if their child went on to a stellar sporting career: sweltering halls, uncomfortable seats and wet feet. Why didn't anyone wear flip-flops any more? They didn't cost much, did they? The man in the suit now approached Jonathan barefoot.

"Hey," he called. "Long time no see."

Jonathan raised his hand in greeting, trying to place the man. There didn't seem to be much muscular substance under the shoulder pads of his jacket, so he didn't appear to be a fellow swimmer. The man came to stand by Jonathan's side.

"Olli," he said, giving Jonathan a quick two-handed slap on the upper arms. "Remember me?"

"Yeah, sure," Jonathan smiled.

The mention of the name had triggered a flood of memories, and amusing episodes began to pour out like coins from a jackpot. Olli Ku... Ko... Keunecke! He had been a few years ahead of Jonathan. The family owned a car dealership. At school, Olli drove used BMWs, flashy on the outside with iridescent high-gloss paint, but with patchy repairs under the hood. In winter, teachers often had to help jumpstart the car after the last lesson. That was the only image Jonathan had of Olli: a pimply young man clamping pliers to the poles of a battery while muttering swear words.

"How are you, man?" Olli asked.

"Fine, and you?"

"Do you still swim?"

Every day. After training, Jonathan would eat a banana and a protein bar. Then he would do two thousand metres of laps, sprints and technical intervals, finishing with a burn-out for arms and legs. He would stagger into the shower, slow and powerless, like an anemone in the current, feeling pleasantly empty inside. At home he would collapse on the sofa, watch TV and then go to bed.

But that wasn't enough for Olli. When asked about "swimming", he meant "winning".

"I don't do competitions any more," Jonathan replied.

"But you used to give it your all."

In his school days, Jonathan had been successful with the team, but on his own he had never made it to the top. He had come close in the two hundred metre backstroke, finishing as runner-up - a word he loathed. It took only a second to say it, the same second Jonathan had missed to win. A tic of the clock, a fraction of a second - when had he wasted those moments? He still didn't know.

"Tension!" Jonathan shouted at Viv. "Give one hundred percent, not ninety. After that we'll just practice starts and then it's time to cool down."

"She's fast, that girl," Olli nodded approvingly. "I wouldn't be able to keep up with her."

"I discovered her," Jonathan said. "She's a great talent."

During the group training sessions, there were always a few children who showed great promise. At the end of each session, Jonathan would assign them extra lanes and have them do stability exercises outside on dry ground. If they completed these exercises without complaining, he would place them in a more advanced group that was currently too strong for them to keep up with. But when he saw the spark of determination in their eyes, when he saw them fighting instead of complaining, Jonathan knew they were promising.

Viv had always stood out. At ten, with long legs, narrow hips and an exceptional feel for the water, she glided ahead of the swarm of her unambitious peers in tournaments, two body lengths ahead of the runner-up by the end of the first lane. After winning two city tournaments, she refused to take part in any minor events. Why sacrifice a day's training for a trivial title? Her slower rivals didn't even challenge her to set new personal bests. The other girls resented her, but Viv didn't care. For her, the thin air at the top was just another source of motivation.

As Viv began her final run, Jonathan hoped Olli would leave soon. Talking to him wouldn't reflect well on Mrs Kaiser.

"How can I help you?" Jonathan asked Olli.

"I want to offer you a job."

"Thanks, but I'm not really into selling."

"No, it's not about cars. I took over the business from my father," Olli waved off casually. "But used cars aren't my thing. People don't want to spend money these days, and it's no fun. So I'm starting a second business."

"Aha?"

Probably import-export, Jonathan thought - buying containers of cheap goods, repackaging them and selling them at inflated prices.

"I'm being supported by the public purse," Olli said.

"Welfare?"

"Ha, that's a good one!" Olli slapped his thighs, laughter echoing off the tiled walls. "No, I work for the job centre. They call themselves an agency now, but it's basically the same old department behind the nameplate."

"You sell cars to them?" Jonathan asked.

"I'm a consultant for European funding initiatives," Olli replied.

"Interesting," Jonathan said hesitantly.

"You have no idea what that means, do you? Nobody does, and that's the good thing," Olli continued. His right trouser leg had rolled down and was hanging in the overflow gutter, but he didn't seem to mind. "I'm designing a new programme to help people with special challenges find work. And it's not about filling in applications or fiddling with Microsoft Office programs - anyone can do that. I prepare people for space."

Jonathan thought he had heard wrong. "Pardon me?"

"For space," Olli repeated.

"Wow," Jonathan replied in surprise.

"And that's why I was looking for you," Olli added.

"But I'm a swimming coach," Jonathan pointed out.

"Never mind. I'm a car salesman," Olli grinned.

"You're pulling my leg."

"It sounds crazy, I know. But let me explain. Just give me another five minutes of your time."

Olli put a hand on Jonathan's back and tried to guide him towards one of the deck chairs.

"I have to finish the training first," Jonathan said, leaning over to Viv who had reached the end of the lane. "Now do ten underwater pulls, Viv!"

Just give me five minutes... It was an old salesman's trick, but what could Jonathan do? Even an unpleasant person should be allowed that little time.

Olli stood close to Jonathan and whispered: "Space exploration is the next big thing. Private initiatives are launching their own satellites, and amateur astronauts are assembling rockets all over the world. Soon, the first ones will be ready to launch. The equipment has become affordable; there are even kits available. Here on Earth, machines are taking over our jobs, which brings us back to the job centre. I ask you: should people still be retrained as cashiers or accountants under these conditions?"

Jonathan shook his head slowly, although he didn't like the way Olli was steering the conversation.

"So what exactly is the space training supposed to look

like?" Olli asked.

That was exactly what Jonathan wanted to know.

"Public funding is not generous, of course," Olli said. "But if anyone can achieve maximum effect with minimum effort, it's me. And don't forget: even the professionals only cook with water. The heat shield of the Soyuz was made of wood. Look it up, it's fascinating. And it did its job. But what will your part be?"

Jonathan swallowed. That would have been his next question. Was Olli a mind reader?

"Astronauts practice external manoeuvres under water," Olli continued. "They use it to simulate weightlessness and slowed movements. They also breathe through a mask, so it's all pretty realistic."

"But I don't have a diving licence," Jonathan replied.

Olli seemed to think for a moment. "Then you'll just snorkel."

"You want me to teach people how to use tools under water?"

"Not just that. Aspiring astronauts need to be physically fit and mentally strong. They need a top coach."

"I don't know..." Jonathan looked in the direction of the entrance. Where was Mrs Kaiser?

"I'm afraid your five minutes are up," he said to Olli. "And I have to turn you down. I don't have time for another job. You can't train an athlete like Viv part-time."

Someone like Olli "Minimal Commitment" Keunecke probably didn't understand the demands of competitive sport. In addition to the hours in the pool, there were just as many hours at the desk, drawing up training plans and analysing competitions. But if you gave it your all, you could be rewarded and end up coaching a swimmer mentioned in the same breath as Ian Thorpe.

"Take my business card," Olli said. "Think about it. Financially, it should be worth it. Fifty per cent more on your current salary is a good deal, isn't it?"

With that offer, he left Jonathan and disappeared towards the changing rooms, his trouser hems dripping.

Jonathan breathed a sigh of relief and raised his right hand, fingers spread, to signal Viv to swim five laps to cool down. And that was that.

But now Mrs Kaiser came. She held shoes and stockings in one hand and a box of chocolates in the other. Seeing the sweets, Jonathan suddenly understood what Viv's mother was going to tell him. He felt like taking a flying leap into the water and diving until his lungs hurt. There was nothing he wanted to see or hear. But being a coward would get him nowhere. So Jonathan stopped and crossed his arms behind his back.

"I wanted to tell you in person," Mrs Kaiser said. "My husband is going to take a management position in Munich, so our family will be moving. This has all happened at very short notice. Thank you for everything you've done for Viv."

Later, Jonathan remembered the box of chocolates in particular, and felt ashamed as he squashed one after another through the cardboard during the conversation. He should have just said "You're welcome" and walked away. Instead, he made a pathetic attempt to force his way into Mrs Kaiser's plans. He offered to move to Munich with them, and it quickly became embarrassing when Mrs Kaiser bluntly told him that they had already hired an American coach for Viv - someone of "top level". That was the exact phrase she had used, and it still echoed in Jonathan's mind as he stood under the hot shower, face to the wall, crying with frustration.

Another coach would accompany Viv to the championships, helping to shape her body with strength exercises and shouting at her before the race: "You can do it! I believe in you!" But for the American, that would just be a worn-out slogan. Only Jonathan really believed in Viv. It took a sharp eye to see the desire to win in a 10-year-old girl, especially when she was unaware of her own.

Despite his influence, Jonathan would probably be forgotten. At most, he might be mentioned in a future biography of Viv, perhaps in a chapter entitled "Athletic Beginnings".

Jonathan drove home, flung his gym bag against the washing machine and dialed Olli's number.

"Sixty percent," he had said. "Give me that, and I'm in."

Heavy sobs ended Jonathan's recollection. At the other end of the line, Viv blew her nose loudly.

"The new coach is an idiot," she complained. "He thinks I'm not training enough. But I can't even sleep anymore because my back muscles are so sore."

"You need to talk to your parents about that," Jonathan said. "All I can say is that I'm still available."

"Mum wouldn't hire you again. For her that would feel like admitting a mistake."

Jonathan looked at his watch. It was ten o'clock. He had nine hours until seven, and he still had music to choose.

"Try to get some sleep," he suggested. "Roll up a blanket and tuck it under your knees. That should take the weight off your back."

3

Christiane Mühlheim, Paula's mother

They shouldn't have thrown her little one out. Bernhard argued that Christiane shouldn't refer to Paula as "little one" because she was already twenty-three. But for Christiane, Paula would always be her baby.

Although Christiane had the day off, she would have preferred to be at the office, where there were distractions. Instead, she wandered around the apartment, wondering what her daughter was up to. Since Paula had left, she'd only phoned twice to say that she was fine and that Christiane shouldn't worry. That was the extent of their conversation. Paula was upset because she felt her parents didn't support her, but Christiane didn't think that was true. After Paula had graduated from high school, Bernhard and Christiane had given her four years to prove that she could make money from her Internet ventures. At first, Paula had played video games, filmed herself, tested cosmetics and later ran a craft blog. Although she claimed to make money from advertising, it wasn't enough to afford her own flat.

Christiane and Bernhard kept encouraging Paula to go to the job centre for advice. Now Paula had finally done so and came back with this incredible story: she was going to be an astronaut! Christiane thought this was nonsense.

Still supportive, Christiane asked if it was an apprenticeship.

"More like training," Paula replied. "When I finish, all doors will be open to me."

This was not how parents imagined the future for their only child. Bernhard told Christiane to stop believing in Paula's unrealistic dreams, otherwise their daughter would still be living with them in her forties instead of becoming independent. Bernhard also worried that if Paula didn't live among ordinary people, they might never have grandchildren

- or they might end up with grandchildren from a weirdo son-in-law.

The day before Paula's astronaut training began, she did this strange thing with her hair.

"Now she's really losing it," Bernhard remarked. "It's time to put our foot down."

As a result, they made her move out and offered her room on Airbnb. Paula could have rented it from them, but she chose not to. Instead, she showed up with a dilapidated van, which she parked on the street with its hazard lights flashing. She loaded a few belongings and then disappeared. The next day, Roger called to say she was staying with him. Roger was a friend of theirs who lived as a drop-out on a fruit farm. Thirty years ago, he had aspired to start a commune, and Bernhard and Christiane had nearly joined him. However, Roger became electrosensitive and disconnected his farm from electricity, making it unappealing for anyone to live there. Occasionally, they would help with the harvest. Paula had often accompanied them, and now she had supposedly parked her van on Roger's property, next to a greenhouse where he grew herbs for the weekly market.

Poor Paula! In addition to her lifelong challenges, she was struggling with a terrible fear of spiders and insects.

Christiane was worried. By now Paula must have realised that the astronaut programme was a scam. As Christiane tidied the flat, she passed Paula's room - the tourist room, as they called it. They had only rented it out once. Christiane found it quite a change to brush her teeth in the morning next to strangers.

Paula's old computer was still on the desk; she had only taken her laptop. Christiane switched it on and started one of the games, but her reactions were too slow. She scrolled through the browser's bookmarks, neatly organised into categories, and quickly found what she was looking for: the online notebook where Paula jotted down her thoughts and ideas. Paula had also encouraged Christiane to try digital notes, but Christiane couldn't get used to it. She preferred to write her shopping lists by hand. Paula's notebook was password-protected.

Christiane stared at the login screen. If only she could see into her daughter's mind! She typed:

"PaulaMühlheim"

It didn't work.

"Password123?"

Wrong again.

How many attempts did she have? If Christiane locked the notebook with too many wrong entries, her snooping would be exposed. But wouldn't Paula be a little pleased to know that her mother was worried? After all, Christiane only had her daughter's best interests at heart.

She noticed a small rubber figure on the screen, a unicorn.

"Unicorn"

Bingo! That was the password!

The title of the latest note was dated the previous day. Christiane opened it and started to read:

Got through my first day as a school bus driver. I was quite nervous before, but now I can drive the van well. At first I was worried about what to do if my hands started shaking and my ears started ringing. I decided that if I felt any signs of panic, I would pull over, pretend I had to go to the toilet and do my breathing exercises behind a tree. After five minutes it would all be over, I could get back behind the wheel and tell myself I was doing fine. The students are lucky I'm picking them up; you can't get anywhere in this area without a car, and to them anyone with a vehicle is a demigod.

My passengers are morning grumblers, slumped in their seats with headphones on, staring out the window at the nothingness of cows and silos.

After dropping them off at school, I have nothing to do until I return at noon. To save fuel, I've parked the van at the school today and walked two kilometres to the shop in the next village. The shop only sells food. I bought bread and apple juice and walked back.

While waiting for the school bell, I decided to do some research. I found out about a private Mars mission online. A foundation wants to send people to set up a colony there, but the catch is that there is no return to Earth. Some experts think this is unethical, but many volunteers have already signed up.

After all, it's not like you can always return in life. Sometimes you inadvertently set a course that can't be corrected. That's why I'm now sitting in a small town less than a hundred kilometres from Jonathan, and the only way I can keep in touch with him is through daily wake-up calls. At least we have that.

4

Paula

On the second day, Emily wanted to get int he van immediately, but I raised my hand.

"Just a moment," I said.

It was seven o'clock on the dot. I parked on the dirt road leading to Emily's house and locked the doors of the van. It must have seemed strange to her, but there was no other way. If I wanted to be on time, I had to make the wake-up call from here.

My mobile phone rang. Jonathan played "I Believe I Can Fly" for me, wished me a good morning and told me to practice nautical knots underwater. He said that it was good for my hand-eye coordination.

I chose "Somewhere Over the Rainbow" and replied that I hadn't found a swimming pool yet, but I would do the knots in my tub.

That was two lies. Firstly, I had found a swimming pool where I took hot showers in the evenings; secondly, I didn't have a bathtub at Roger's rotten place.

I would have liked to ask Jonathan how he was, but I was afraid that if I let my guard down he would ask me where I was and if he could come and see me. But that would only have been possible in the dark. I couldn't look him in the eye.

We said goodbye and I put my phone down before I opened Emily's door.

Instead of asking me about the secret conversation I had just had, the girl dropped into her seat without a word. I noticed that her jacket was damp.

"I'm sorry to have kept you waiting," I said. "But I'm afraid I can't let you in until five past seven."

This mysterious remark didn't arouse her curiosity. I stepped on the gas and thought about what I could talk to her about. I had no mobile phone reception at Roger's because the oddball had a court order prohibiting the erection of transmission masts in his immediate vicinity. Reading had been my only evening activity for days and I was in desperate need of low-level entertainment, gossip and a bit of girl talk.

"Are you an artist?" I asked Emily.

"Why?" she replied, looking at me in horror, as if I'd asked her if she had terminal syphilis.

"Because you're dressed in black," I said, "and there are canvases in your garden."

"Those are my mother's things. I hate artists."

"Yes," I said. "They can be annoying."

Her face lit up and she pulled a card out of her rucksack.

"I want to be a mathematician. I started a vlog last year where I solve problems and explain formulas. I already have nearly 9,000 subscribers."

"Not bad." I pocketed the card.

Emily nodded in satisfaction, but then fell silent again. There was no way we were going to get a conversation going like this. I decided to Google some maths problems later.

"Being able to do maths is important for me too," I said. "Because I'm going to be an astronaut."

"Really?"

Finally, she was interested in me. Under her admiring gaze, I felt myself grow a few centimetres. You're a hero to this girl, I thought. Not only do you drive and have a car, you also work in a glamorous job. You're a role model, so you have to be careful what you say.

"It was surprisingly easy to get started," I said. "I got on the programme through the job centre."

When my parents had asked me for the thousandth time to finally make an appointment for counselling, I had agreed for the sake of peace. Little did I know that they would evict me soon after.

Before the appointment I thought about the whole thing. I didn't want to just go in and be a run-of-the-mill customer. Anyone who makes money online knows how important it is to target your audience. I needed to find out what the advisers wanted. So I asked my mate Nino, a hacker, if he could find out about the really good jobs, the ones that weren't listed on the website.

Nino thought I was being silly, but being the curious tinkerer that he is, he spent a whole evening poking around on poorly secured servers. Finally, he wrote to me that there was an astronaut programme for autistic people.

I did a bit of research and practised in the mirror, looking down quickly when I made eye contact with myself and making nervous movements with my fingers. At first I felt guilty about my preparations, but then I told myself: What support programmes are there for people who sometimes feel overwhelmed with anxiety for no reason and struggle to get out of bed for a few days every year?

Apart from the medication the paediatrician shouldn't have prescribed me at the time - pills that turned me into a fluffy, mossy stone that could bang its shins on furniture without feeling any pain - my anxiety hadn't done me any good. It was time for mental illness to give something back!

The counsellor assigned to me, Mr Schwarz, was difficult to deal with. My attempts at acting had no effect at first. I had to sort the pamphlets on his desk by colour and look around desperately until he finally asked me if everything was all right.

"I'm sorry," I said. "It's just that I need order and I feel uncomfortable in unfamiliar surroundings at first."

Even then his bell didn't ring.

"I am a person with special needs and talents," I said.

He leafed through the copies of school reports I had brought. "I see you got average grades in all subjects except physical education. That's not so special."

"What about not leaving my room for months?"

This was almost true. My mother did most of the shopping and I only went out occasionally for snacks. To manage this, I wore dark sunglasses and used a service for the blind where I gave my shopping list to an assistant who walked me through the aisles. With this help, I was able to resist the urge to buy on impulse.

Slowly it dawned on the Mr Schwarz.

"Let me have a quick word with a colleague."

He disappeared for a moment and returned with a piece of paper with another room number and a name on it.

I had an easier time with Mrs Bunte. She was visibly pleased to see me and spoke enthusiastically about the "great programme" with an "open concept". The whole thing was to start the following week.

On my first day in the program, several things became clear to me. The office had obviously struggled to find genuine autistic people. Perhaps most of them already had jobs? In any case, apart from two men playing chess against each other in their minds, the other participants didn't strike me as unusual.

We had been directed to an address in an industrial estate. I had to walk almost two kilometers from the bus stop. Finally, I stood in front of a warehouse that looked like a place where the mafia might lure in members they suspected of betrayal. Inside, ten people were already sitting in a circle of chairs. There were two blondes in identical leggings and shirts depicting the silhouette of a ballerina, a chubby red-haired lady in a flowing blouse dress, and an elderly gentleman in a suit. Beside the mind chess players, four other men made themselves small in their chairs, looking as if they would rather be somewhere else.

Everyone was staring at me, and I started to sweat, which felt quite uncomfortable while wearing a swimming cap. I didn't want to touch my head and scratch it because that would probably make them stare even more.

Only Mr. Schwarz, who already knew my story, acted as if my appearance was completely normal. He explained that he was filling in for the head of the program, who was unfortunately unable to attend due to another important appointment.

"We're all set now," he said. "The coaches are running a little late because they need to gather some materials."

Next, we were supposed to introduce ourselves. The man in the suit shared that he had been a quality controller for hardwood floors until the company he worked for went bankrupt. Now, at over fifty years old, he was struggling to find a new job. His area of interest was antique toy collecting, and he was knowledgeable in that field. The counselor nodded and mentioned something about "self-employment" and a "business plan."

The blondes - surprise, surprise - wanted to be dancers, but they also wanted to train as actors to have an alternative career when they got older and their bodies couldn't keep up. After they had talked for ten minutes, Mr Schwarz tried to interrupt them, but to no avail.

"Coffee break," he finally announced.

On a folding table against the wall, next to a calcified sink, were plastic cups, spoons, a bowl of tea bags, jars of instant coffee powder and cream, and a kettle. I began to wonder if this programme was as great as they claimed, especially as they had already cut costs on the venue and equipment.

"The coaches," Mr Schwarz called. "Finally!"

Two women and Jonathan walked in.

I thought, BOOM!

Jonathan was wearing white trainers, plain grey trousers, a black t-shirt and a diving watch on his left wrist. His eyes looked slightly puffy. He had shaved his face and head.

I had never liked bald heads, but that changed in an instant. Hair seemed unnecessary on Jonathan. From his feet to his scalp he was smooth and perfect - someone could have carved him out of stone. I felt a warmth inside. How I would have loved to rest my forehead on this man's neck!

And the best part? This gorgeous guy was coming straight at me. He crossed the hall, stopped in front of me and smiled as if we were old friends meeting again after a long time.

"Hello," he said. "I'm Jonathan."

I reached out to shake his hand, forgetting that I was holding a spoon because I was about to make a drink. Coffee cream dripped onto the floor like stardust.

Emily leaned forward.

"Did the job centre place you directly with the European Space Agency?" she asked.

"No, we went through a sort of training course," I replied. "On the first day we were given laptops and told to read about the history of space travel."

Emily looked bored.

"And I fell in love with the coach," I added.

She looked interested again.

"But then you got cancer?" she pressed.

"No," I said, feeling offended. The swimming cap wasn't meant to make me look sick.

"Then what happened to your hair?" she asked.

"I'll tell you on the way back."

We were almost at my second passenger's house and I didn't want to share this embarrassing episode with more than one person.

"Today I'm attending the research club in the afternoon," Emily said. "Afterwards, I'm being picked up by a friend's father. Will you tell me tomorrow?"

"We'll see." I gave her a sideways glance. "Can you give me the password for the school Wi-Fi?"

If I didn't download some movies soon, I was going to die of boredom.

"Deal," Emily replied.

5

Jonathan

"Somewhere Over the Rainbow" - what was Paula trying to tell Jonathan with that song? Was it an allusion to their refusal to wake up from their dream? They were like drunken fools who wouldn't take off their carnival costumes on Ash Wednesday. They still pretended that Paula was an astronaut and that Jonathan was a ground control employee.

But the programme had ended before it had really begun. Jonathan shouldn't have trusted Olli; someone like him was only interested in his own advantage. Little did Olli know the disappointment he had caused the hopeful participants. Jonathan understood why Paula had withdrawn after bragging to everyone she knew about her astronaut training.

All Jonathan could do was wait until Paula was ready to meet him again. At least she didn't blame him for the failure of the programme. Olli had disappeared. At his car dealership, Jonathan was told that the boss was on holiday. Did Olli really think he could steal money, blame it on Jonathan and get away with it?

Jonathan's return to his old life was blocked. He'd given his children's swimming groups to colleagues and wouldn't be getting them back. The children's swimming programme was co-financed by the city, and Mrs Bunte had threatened that Jonathan would never get another publicly funded job. He might be able to keep the triathlon preparation group going privately, but the participants had annoyed him for a long time with their know-it-all attitude. Each of them acted like an expert on the latest equipment and the best supplements. When Jonathan told them to leave their smartwatches at home and just concentrate on covering distance in the water, they rolled their eyes.

Jonathan decided to go to Munich and check on Viv. Her call had worried him more than he liked to admit. That night he had lain awake wondering about her threat to kill herself.

Eventually he got up and found a ride south.

He would meet two students at the bus station at ten. There was a good hour left before that. Just as he was about to make himself a second cup of tea to relieve his hangover, the phone rang. It was his father, and he sounded desperate.

"I can't find my pills," he said.

"Where did you last see them?" Jonathan asked.

"On the living room table. The tin was next to the remote control. Maybe it fell and rolled under a piece of furniture."

Jonathan groaned. The tin might have fallen, but it was unlikely to have rolled under the furniture. That wasn't possible in his father's flat. The old man had lived alone since Jonathan's mother had died. Although he got on well with a lady from the allotment society, it wasn't likely to develop into anything serious. Jonathan's father avoided inviting people over for good reason.

"I'll come," Jonathan said.

His bike would get him to his father's and then to the bus station in time. But as soon as he unlocked his parents' front door, he noticed something new. Despite the cluttered hallway with its piles of magazines, bulging suitcases and boxes, something caught his attention. Perhaps it was his subconscious that had alerted him. If one were to fully perceive every impression, the mind would be overwhelmed, especially in his father's small three-room apartment.

Jonathan had offered to help clean several times, but each attempt had ended with them sorting things instead. Piles of clothes, stacks of boxes and towers of books filled the rooms, and nothing was ever thrown away.

"You've bought stuff again," Jonathan said in exasperation.

Stuck between a wardrobe and a collection of wine crates in the far left corner was a bin bag that hadn't been there on his last visit. When Jonathan tried to lift it, the plastic ripped and something inside clinked.

"Plant pots," his father said cheerfully. "I went to the charity flea market where you can take anything for a donation.

I couldn't leave these beautiful pots behind. Some of them are hand-painted. And if I ever want to grow vegetables on the balcony..."

"Where on the balcony?" Jonathan asked incredulously.

Although he tried to remain calm, a familiar frustration washed over him every time he saw how overwhelmed his father was.

"There's no room!"

He felt like a poor coach, unable to help his own father. He had tried gentle methods, such as following the advice of a book by a Japanese organisation expert who suggested picking up every object and assessing whether it brought joy. That didn't get them very far. Jonathan's father was grateful for all his possessions, no matter how trivial, and found absurd uses for even the most junky items.

In a desperate attempt, Jonathan had taken advantage of his father's doctor's appointment to take a trunk full of stuff to the dump with two friends. They hurriedly stuffed things into boxes without sorting them. The effect was minimal. They only managed to clear three square metres.

"What are you missing now?" Jonathan asked his father on his return.

The old man didn't know. He couldn't name a single part. But there seemed to be a sense of loss that he had immediately filled by acquiring more items the very next day.

Jonathan followed the tracks. There were only certain paths left in the flat, narrow trails that led to the cooker and the fridge, the television chair and the bed. His father's pills had probably been lost in one of these places, but with him standing chest high among the hoarded items, this limitation was not helpful. Jonathan tried his luck in the kitchen, rummaging through a shopping basket by the stove. Inside he found shopping lists, bottles of cleaning products and corks. Then, further down in the basket, his fingers brushed against something smooth. His heart leapt with hope, but when he pulled it out, it turned out to be a rubber glove.

For a moment Jonathan thought he had touched Paula's bathing cap. He remembered the first day of the astronaut programme when he had walked into the hall and seen Paula in her green cap. Suddenly it all made sense: Jonathan's semi-successful career as a swimmer, the countless kids from the junior groups he had tried to motivate but lost after a few months to dancing, boxing or tennis, and the humiliating dismissal as Viv's coach that had come with cheap chocolate. All this had happened so that he could meet this enchanting woman that morning.

He had sacrificed a lot for his sport, but even he had never thought of walking around in shorts and flip-flops in the summer. Outside the pool, he always dressed "appropriately". But why? Wasn't it just a question of having the courage to show the world that he was a swimmer? Basketball shoes and tennis socks had been in fashion for a while, and Jonathan interpreted Paula's cap as an ironic comment on those fashion trends. He liked women with a sense of humour.

Jonathan and the other two coaches had expected Olli to turn up to say a few words of introduction, but he didn't. Mrs Bunte from the agency finally organised laptops so that the participants could continue their training online, but there weren't enough devices. The girls who wanted to be dancers suggested going to the library, which they were allowed to do. Judging by their happy faces, they seemed eager to go home.

Jonathan introduced himself to the group as a swimming coach and announced that he would start the practical part of the training the following day at 7am in the indoor pool. Two men claimed to be allergic to chlorine and the others looked unenthusiastic. Only Paula promised to be there.

"If not you, who else?" Jonathan said.

Now that he had only her to focus on, they sat down with a laptop, a bit away from the others.

"So what now?" Paula asked.

"Let's learn about astronauts," Jonathan replied. "I know as little about the job as you do."

The European Space Agency's requirements were lower than either of them had thought. To be considered as an astronaut, you had to be between 27 and 37 years old (Paula was still too young), between 153 and 190 centimetres tall (she was 169 centimetres) and be able to speak and write English.

"Yes, sir," Paula replied.

You should also have studied and ideally worked in science or been a pilot.

"I can still do both," Paula replied.

There was a hint of irony in her voice, but Jonathan looked at her seriously.

"Why not?"

Until he had met Paula, Jonathan had mainly wanted to do this job to distract himself from his disappointment with Viv. He hadn't believed for a second that one of the participants might actually go into space one day. He thought the programme was an interesting idea that someone had conceived, only to be constrained by hundreds of rules and regulations, resulting in a poor version of the original plan. Listless participants and overworked supervisors would eventually kill the vision.

But it was not impossible. Sitting next to Jonathan was a young woman in a swimming cap. What could stop her? Jonathan felt energised. He remembered his days as an active sportsman: training until he could barely muster the strength to lift himself over the side of the pool. Three days before a competition, he would reduce his workload and then, standing on the starting block, rested and full of pent-up energy, he was suddenly capable of more than he thought possible.

As Jonathan's mind wandered, he searched his bedroom, ploughing through the pile of laundry in front of the bed with arm movements that resembled a breaststroke, and just as he was about to give up and move on to the next room, he grabbed a small box through the pocket of a cardigan.

"I've got the pills, Dad!"
"Oh, son, you're a gem."

The gem looked up at the clocks on the wall, two of which were still running. They showed five past ten. Jonathan's ride was gone.

6
Emily

At 6.30am, Paula pulled the van into the driveway. From the kitchen window, Emily watched as the young woman wrapped herself in a blanket and opened her laptop. Now that Paula had the Wi-Fi key, she was probably busy with astronaut-related tasks like calculating trajectories.

Emily made coffee, poured it into a thermos and took her time with breakfast. When the clock struck seven, Paula picked up the phone and talked for four minutes. Emily kept an eye on her and did not leave the house until Paula was finished.

"I've brought you something warm to drink," Emily said, handing Paula the thermos.

"Thanks, that's nice of you," Paula replied, taking a sip. "Off to school then."

"Who are you always talking to on the phone?" Emily asked.

"I'm talking to the ground station." Paula slipped a finger under the brim of her bathing cap to scratch her head. "Do you think I'm crazy?"

"No, why would I?"

"Well, technically I'm just a school bus driver."

"But you could go into space one day."

"Theoretically, yes."

"Well, there you go. My mother once painted a picture of a tree house. She found a huge canvas, four by three metres, for cheap because a shop was going out of business. For weeks she talked about doing something special with it. When she finally started painting, I didn't notice at first. It took her a whole month to finish, and when it was done she wanted me to admire it. Her friends were crazy about it, raving about the vibrant colours and how realistic it looked. But I was annoyed. She could have built a real tree house back then. We both would have benefited. Acrylic on canvas - what's the point?"

Emily snorted angrily. "I hate artists!"

"I see," Paula said. "But it's important to get on with the people you depend on. Communication is the key. If it doesn't work, the whole mission could fail. Arguments between the astronauts and ground control are the worst thing that can happen. That's why there are wake-up calls to ensure a good atmosphere. During the first call of the day, ground control plays a song and sends greetings from the astronauts' friends and family. The crew on the space station also responds with music and personal messages. Only then do they discuss science and upcoming experiments and manoeuvres."

"Who is your ground station?" Emily asked.

"A swimming coach called Jonathan."

"Is that why you wear the swim cap?"

"No, I had it before I met him."

"I see."

Emily didn't want to dwell on the subject. Fashion, like art, was an area she found overly fussy. A friend of her mother's had worn nothing but blankets last winter, draped around her like a toga and held in place with safety pins. It looked absolutely silly. The friend claimed the blankets were Peruvian ponchos, but Emily had seen a laundry list with furniture logos printed on it.

"I wanted to ask you something," Emily said. "Can I interview you for my vlog?"

"Me? Why?"

"Because you're a great example of what you can achieve if you're good at maths."

7

Paula

Me being good at maths? Haha! I'm more of a hands-on kind of person. While that helps when I'm converting ingredients for baking recipes, it could be fatal in space. Even a small deviation can send a satellite off course. The Mars orbiter was lost because the Americans and Europeans were using different units of measurement and the discrepancy was noticed too late. The data probably looked fine at first.

The pixie haircut I saw in an online magazine the day before the astronaut programme started looked good too. I had been searching my wardrobe for an outfit that looked both professional and stylish, and as I tried different combinations, my hair became a mess that was driving me crazy. I needed a new haircut! But it was too late to go to the salon. Then I saw a photo of an elfish woman with a pixie cut, supposedly the trendy hairstyle of the year. Short at the back, long bangs at the front, styled to the side - I thought I could do that myself. I decided to use my dad's clippers for the back and scissors for the front.

My first attempt came close to the original look, but then I made the mistake of trying to touch up a few areas and suddenly there were gaps in my hair. The back was beyond repair and the fringe was looking strange. I bravely cut everything down to two centimetres, but now the stubble was sticking out and couldn't be tamed even with wax. My head looked like a dishwashing brush. I tried to hide it with various hats and scarves, but my first impression in the mirror always reminded me of a chemotherapy patient. Near despair, I grabbed a bathing cap and finally felt good again. Now I looked like an athlete on my way to training. The only inconvenience was putting the cap on and taking it off, because it pulled my hair. So I decided to shave my head bald. Once it was all off, I felt relieved. I like to do things thoroughly, even if it means making a complete mess.

Emily interrupted my thoughts. "So, what do you think? May I interview you?"

"I'll think about it. But I'm sure you could find more interesting people than me. After all, I'm only in a training programme. It's uncertain if I'll ever be selected for a mission."

"It's the same with all astronauts."

"Honestly, I would fail the psychological test."

"Why?"

"Because of fear."

"Fear is a normal feeling."

"But only in dangerous situations. Sometimes I get scared for no apparent reason."

"What do you do then?"

"I concentrate on my breathing."

"Nothing else?"

"No. Adrenaline doesn't last long in the body. After a few minutes the fear usually passes."

"Be glad. There are worse things. My mother gets flashes of inspiration that last for days."

We were approaching the second stop. As soon as more students got on, Emily fell silent. Either she didn't like the others, or she wanted to keep my story to herself. She pulled a pair of headphones out of the pocket of her hoodie.

"Think about it," she said.

8

Christiane Mühlheim, Paulas Mutter

Christiane had received a request for the room, but she turned it down and deleted the email so that Bernhard would not notice. At that moment, her main concern was to find out what Paula was doing. There was this strange mention of a Mars mission, and Christiane was disturbed by Paula's belief that she couldn't correct her course.

Because Roger didn't have a telephone line, Christiane couldn't reach him. When he needed to make a call, he went to the post office. Christiane had left a message there asking him to contact her immediately. But he hadn't replied yet.

To keep up with Paula, Christiane used the computer in Paula's former room. Every morning and evening she had a look at the online notebook. Finally, there was a new entry:

"Should I let Emily interview me? I could talk about my first day of training. If I had known that it would also be my last day with Jonathan, I would have taken photos or made a video to capture every detail.

I arrived at the pool at seven o'clock and was waiting shivering in the passageway between the large and small pools when Jonathan walked in with a bag slung over his shoulder.

"Are you cold? I've got something for you," he said as he handed me a pile of white T-shirts. I was going to take just one, but he shook his head and laughed.

"Put them all on, one on top of the other. We're simulating the restricted movement of a space suit."

"But I'm not a good swimmer. If these get wet, I'll sink," I protested.

"You're not supposed to swim, you're supposed to walk."

"Then why are we here? We could do this outside."

"Walk underwater, I mean. You're going to walk across the bottom of the pool with a weight belt and a snorkel."

"You want to kill me!"

"Would it calm you down if I jumped into the pool with you?"

"Not particularly."

"I'll do it anyway."

He put his bag on the side of the pool, took out a mask and snorkel, and put on the equipment as if it were the most normal thing in the world. I struggled with the mask's elastic strap, which didn't fit comfortably over or under my ears.

"Pull it over the top of your ear," Jonathan advised. "That's where it holds best. May I help?"

He showed me. "And now you put the snorkel here..."

Another expert move. To do something, I bit the rubber bead of the mouthpiece and tried two breaths.

"Don't pant," Jonathan said. "Just breathe in and out normally."

On the steps leading down to the non-swimmer section of the pool, we put on weight belts. Mine had an extra loop with a screwdriver in it. Before I could ask Jonathan what to do with it, he showed me a pegboard with a row of screws.

"Astronauts have to make repairs. It takes practice in zero gravity."

Hesitantly, I entered the water up to my knees. It seemed barely heated. On the other side of the pool, three figures dressed in black were doing their laps.

"Why aren't we wearing wetsuits?" I asked.

"What they're wearing are triathlon suits, they don't keep you warm. Besides, I didn't want to overwhelm you with too much equipment."

"Better to be overwhelmed than frozen to death."

"Come on, just keep moving and you'll warm up."

He rushed past me down the steps, threw himself into the water and dived under. Apart from his frantic paddling movements, there was nothing to suggest he was cold.

I took a deep breath, tucked my head between my shoulders and jumped in after him. Indeed, getting in had been the hardest part. In this part of the pool, the water was only up to my chest, but I made myself small so that as little of me as possible was exposed to the air. In the water, the different layers of clothing flowed around my body like seaweed, but as soon as I stood up straight and my shoulders were in the air, the soaked cotton stuck to me and pulled me down.

This was the moment when I could have panicked and Jonathan would probably have understood. I listened to my inner voice, but it was silent.

"We'll practise walking first," Jonathan said.

He took three swimming tyres from his bag, which were attached to weights with cords, and lowered them into the swimming area of the pool. The tyres were now half a metre under water.

Jonathan told me to go underwater, breathe through the snorkel and carry the swimming tyres from one end of the pool to the other. He demonstrated it. Then I tried it. It wasn't difficult, in fact it was reassuring because the resistance of the water forced me to move slowly, like in Tai Chi. I walked back and forth and began to enjoy it. It was not a hostile environment. The water carried me. Air flowed into my lungs through the tube of the snorkel as if I were on land, and all I had to do was release the weight belt to float gently upwards. The silence was wonderful too. I got into a flow and can't remember how many times I carried the tyres around the pool. At one point Jonathan's hand appeared in front of my face and signalled for me to stop.

I pushed myself off the bottom and surfaced.

"Very nice," he said. "You're doing a great job. It's like you've never done anything else. Ready for the next level?"

I mumbled agreeing, still holding the snorkel in my mouth.

"Here's the situation: you're aboard the space station. The automatic monitoring system reports a leak in the airlock. It cannot be repaired from the inside. So you have to go outside."

He took the pegboard with the screws, jumped into the pool, swam to the centre and sank the pegboard there. Then he swam back to me. I admired his style. His gliding through the water was so effortless.

"It's not difficult to unscrew the screws," he said when he was back with me. "But make sure you don't let go of your tool or any of the screws you've removed. There is no gravity in space, they would drift away. All right? Let's go."

I went underwater to the board. Once there, I took the screwdriver from my belt with my right hand. With my free left hand I held the board while I turned the screw. When most of the screw was out, it got tricky. I had to release my hand from the board in time to catch the screw. But as soon as I let go, I could no longer turn the screw because the board would drift around without any support. It took me three attempts to get it right. Where to put the screw now? I squeezed it between my little right finger and the screwdriver. I also managed to loosen the second screw, but by the time I had almost removed the third from the board, my fingers were aching from the effort. I wanted to tighten the screw again so that I could think about it in a little more peace. But I couldn't manage to turn the tool in the opposite direction. My brain gave the command, but my hand didn't know what to do. This was the kind of failure I knew from physical education.

Although I was breathing faster, hardly any air seemed to be reaching my lungs. My head felt light. My chest felt like a balloon. One leg got caught in the string that held the board to the weight and then it was over. I began to struggle, not knowing which way was up and which way was down. When I took my next breath, water filled my mouth. I separated my lips from the rubber bead of the mouthpiece and screamed. But the sound only reached my own ears.

Jonathan grabbed my arms and pulled me to the edge of the pool. He told me that later, I didn't realise. The next thing I remember is sitting on the tiles at the edge of the pool, looking in amazement at the fingerprints above my elbows.

"What was going on?" Jonathan asked.

"I panicked. The screws, the tools, the board... I didn't

know how to continue."

As I said this, I realised that I was still holding the screws in my hands.

"You could have just let go," Jonathan said.

"But then the screws would have drifted away and I wouldn't have completed my mission."

"Paula, it was just an exercise!"

"But in space you wouldn't have been there to save me. I would have died."

Jonathan looked at me with what I thought was a spark of admiration.

"Right?" I followed up. "In space it would have been over for me."

"If you breathe water, you can die in a swimming pool," he said.

I nodded. The triathletes were still swimming their laps, paying no attention to us. They were all fighting for themselves. But even if they'd seen my battle with the board, they wouldn't have understood what it meant to me. Jonathan had no idea either. For the first time in a long time, I was scared in a real dangerous situation. That was great progress.

9

Emily

Emily was in the back seat of the driving school car, pointing her cousin Nele in the direction of the city. Nele was going on a cross-country trip and the driving instructor had allowed Emily to come along and choose the destination, as long as it was no more than 45 minutes away. So Emily was going to visit Jonathan.

She had found the website that told her when to meet him at the pool.

On the way back from school, Paula had told Emily why she was wearing the bathing cap. Emily was disappointed. She had hoped there would be a spectacular reason for Paula's hairlessness, such as plutonium poisoning or an injury to her skull. But a failed attempt at self-trimming? How boring. Paula was only ten years older than Emily, but she seemed to be the kind of adult who was always thinking about the past. Paula's mother liked to tell the story of how she had already secured a place at an art school in England and then got pregnant. So what? Who cared?

Emily was determined to interview Paula. So far she had only had one guest on her vlog, her maths teacher. He had been visibly uncomfortable in front of the camera and had stuttered. But a future astronaut would bring in new followers, provided Paula had interesting things to say about her training. If all she did was drive a school bus twice a day, that wouldn't be the case. That's why the coach was needed.

Emily consulted the route planner on her mobile phone.

"Take the next exit," she said, "and then turn right again at the next opportunity."

"Look at that, a roundabout," the driving instructor said. "You've chosen a nice route, Emily. Please do two laps on the inside, Nele, we haven't practised that yet."

"Great. Thank you, Emily," Nele said.

Emily grinned. "Sorry. I hope there's a nice, big car park."

But there was only one narrow parking space in front of the pool.

"Perfect for practising," Emily said. "I'll just get out while you squeeze in. Be right back."

She ran to the door of the pool. From the foyer, a window looked out onto the large pool. A group of children were doing the backstroke in separate lanes. But the coach was a woman.

Emily asked the man at the ticket counter about Jonathan.

"He doesn't work here any more," he said. "Would you like to join one of the groups? There are still places available on Wednesdays."

Emily said no, thanked him and ran back outside where Nele was doing a parking manoeuvre. When Emily got in, she was sweating and cursing.

There were ten minutes left in the lesson. That should be enough. The address Emily had found in an online phone book was nearby.

"We'll take a little detour back to the motorway," Emily said. "One without roundabouts, okay?"

"Very considerate of you," Nele said. "Otherwise I would have given you a lift for the last time."

Jonathan's flat was in a block of eight. Emily rang the doorbell.

What was she going to say when he opened the door? She had assumed that at the mention of Paula, Jonathan would grab his jacket and come with her. But now, standing at his door, Emily doubted it. If Jonathan wanted to see Paula, he could just go and see her. After all, they spoke on the phone every day. But obviously there was a reason why they had broken up and Paula was now living in the car. Was it Paula's fault? She was the one who had left town.

No one answered the door. Emily rang a second time and stepped back from the front door. Jonathan's doorbell was the second lowest, and if that corresponded to the location of the flat, he wasn't home. Only the top two floors of the five-storey block had lights on.

How stupid, Emily thought. You drive thirty kilometres and then the rocket can't take off because the ground crew didn't turn up for work.

10

Jonathan

Jonathan was lucky. His ride's car had to be repaired due to a broken fan belt, postponing the trip for a day. While waiting at the bus station, Jonathan searched for a song for the next morning.

Thank God he had mentioned the wake-up calls.

After training in the indoor pool, he and Paula had eaten fried noodles and talked at a nearby kiosk. It had been a long time since Jonathan had chatted so casually on a first date. But this wasn't a date, it was a work meeting, even if Jonathan's heart was beating fast.

Paula was still wearing her bathing cap, but that was the only thing that was noticeable about her. In his preparation for the programme, Jonathan had read that autistic people don't understand irony, and rather than address this directly, he talked to Paula about misunderstandings between astronauts from different cultural backgrounds and disputes between crews and ground control. When he mentioned the tradition of wake-up calls, Paula said she thought it was a nice idea and suggested they could do the same. They exchanged phone numbers. Jonathan said the success of the mission was the most important thing. Paula grinned and replied: "Yes, exactly."

Then they drove to the hall where the other two coaches, Mrs Schwanitz and Mrs Adelcu, were writing CVs with the participants.

Mrs Adelcu took Jonathan aside. "Have you heard from Mr Keunecke?" she asked.

"No, not today."

"Where is he? He was supposed to present the concept, there was talk of different training modules to which experts would be invited. Yesterday, Mr Keunecke told us that the experts were still at an important congress. So we're covering for them today. But we can't wait another day".

"I don't know anything. I've been hired for the sports part, and unfortunately only one participant wants to attend."

"How unfortunate for you." Mrs Adelcu looked at Jonathan suspiciously. Could she see into his head? Or was she just jealous that he had spent the morning in the swimming pool while she had been stuck in the drafty hall?

"Make sure you get the laptops back today," she said. "They can't stay in the hall as the door is poorly secured."

"No problem, I'll take care of it."

Jonathan spoke lightly, believing it would only take him fifteen minutes to drive past the Job Centre on his way home. He hadn't expected to run into Ollie at all. If only he'd avoided that encounter, he wouldn't be in trouble now.

But Jonathan had been the last one in the hall. He was just carrying the boxes of charging cables to his car and planning his own evening training session (long distance, a hundred laps at a steady pace) when a red BMW pulled up to the side of the road and Ollie got out.

"Hey, how's it going?"

Ollie wore dirty trainers and greasy jeans, but a spotless white shirt and a watch that was recognisable from a distance. Apparently, when he had dressed, he had assumed that he would only be seen from the waist up - through the rolled down driver's window.

"Good," Jonathan said. "I've only got one swimmer, but she's very motivated. She almost drowned today because she wouldn't let go of the screws during a repair exercise."

"Wonderful. Speaking of which, I'll bring you the sports budget."

"Why budget? I get a salary from the agency."

"That's what I'm supposed to do, but it involves forms and administration." Olli shook his hands as if he had touched something disgusting. "I work with cash. There's always petty cash if you ask nicely. I'll pay you now, in advance. Because I like you."

Ollie reached behind him and handed Jonathan a brown

envelope. Had he taken it from his waistband?

"Let's do this the official way," Jonathan said. "There's still so much to be deducted."

"Are you afraid I'll miss out? I've already pocketed the amount I'm entitled to for the planning."

"I was talking about deductions for social security and tax. But for the planning: Mrs Adelcu missed you today."

"Her! You should forget her. She's set in her ways and lacks inspiration. It didn't suit her to be given the job here."

"Well, the facilities are a bit special. I'm in the pool half the time, but she..."

"She should be happy to see something new. How are you supposed to get into the space mood in the stuffy rooms of the agency?" Ollie hummed the intro to "Star Wars" and ended with a noise. "You know what they say: think outside the box."

"Except this box is pretty drafty. But sort it out between you two."

"I have nothing to do with her anymore. That's why I want to give you the money. You have to pay for using the pool, don't you?"

Ollie pressed the envelope against Jonathan's chest, but Jonathan still didn't take it.

"Mrs Bunte should deal with the manager," he said. "I don't want to be involved in administrative stuff."

"You're right," Ollie said. "But we both know how it is. If you have to go through official channels, aliens might land before you get anything approved. Look, it's simple: I'll put your money in the first-aid box at the back of the hall. If you need it ..."

"Whatever. Do what you want. I have to get the laptops out of here and then off to training."

"See you."

That should have been the last thing Jonathan heard from Ollie, but at that point he had no idea. He drove to the agency, dropped off the laptops, drove home, ate a banana and a yoghurt and jumped on his bike to get to his own training session on time.

On the way and in the water, he thought about the music for his first wake-up call. It had to be light, but catchy. Did Paula like musicals? West Side Story? But that was too much heartache to start with. Phantom of the Opera? Too dramatic. At the turn to lane 98, Jonathan had an idea: he would play something from the soundtrack of "2001: A Space Odyssey".

He left the pool humming.

"Psst!"

He turned. A figure crouched beside the bike racks.

"Paula?"

Jonathan's heart, though tired from the endurance training, went into sprint mode again.

"Interesting who you're hoping to see," a voice said.

In the light of a street lamp, Jonathan recognised Mrs Adelcu.

"What are you doing here?" Jonathan asked.

"Waiting for you. For an hour."

"You'd see me at work tomorrow."

"Not at the moment. I'm on strike. Over the years I've heard a lot of silly ideas from young people who thought they had to turn the training department upside down. But this space thing takes the cake. And Mr Keunecke is a windbag".

She was right. Ollie really wasn't a trustworthy person. But without him, Jonathan would probably never have met Paula.

"Outside input can be enriching," Jonathan said.

"What a load of rubbish! And autistic people? Who here is autistic?"

"It's not written on anyone's forehead. But those two who play chess in their minds..."

"Yes, maybe they are. They might have Asperger's syndrome. But not all of them are gifted. Just like not all boys can play football."

Why was she looking at Jonathan now?

"Exactly," he said. "That's why I became a swimmer."

"A dull sport."

"Good evening, Mrs Adelcu. I'm going home now."

"Sorry about that. I'm just frustrated at all the time I've wasted, and I've got a stiff neck from the draught in the hall."

"But then you probably want to go home."

"I don't understand why Mr Keunecke wants to work for us. What does he get out of it?"

"I can't answer that question." Jonathan got on his bike. "And now I have to replenish my carbohydrate reserves, because in 22 hours I have another mindless training session. Bye."

He pushed off and pedalled with every ounce of strength his legs could muster. Riding fast felt a bit like flying. The wind blew in his face and a cloud of aroma from the nearby coffee roastery invigorated him. Jonathan looked forward to the next morning.

Friday started with a shock. Jonathan's phone rang at half past six. It was Mrs Bunte from the agency. She said there had been a misunderstanding about the budget. Mr Keunecke had received cash, which was completely unusual and due to a mistake in the process.

Her language was awkward, and Jonathan didn't immediately understand what she was getting at. But when he tried to get rid of her, because he didn't want to keep Paula waiting, Mrs Bunte made herself clearer.

The money had to be paid back. Mr Keunecke claimed to have left it all in the hall.

"The money is still there," Jonathan said. "I didn't want it. As you say yourself, it's unusual ..."

Mrs Bunte cut him off with a torrent of angry words, giving him no opportunity to defend himself.

The money was gone, she had seen for herself. Jonathan was conspiring with Mr. Keunecke. Even if she couldn't prove that he had embezzled the budget, he would do well to return it immediately. Otherwise, she would use her contacts to have

Jonathan banned from all city-funded jobs until he retired. In other words, no more children's training groups for him.

The astronaut programme was also put on hold until further notice. All participants would be informed.

A small car stopped in front of the bus platform. The window was down.

"Drive to Munich?" the driver asked. "Are you Jonathan?"

Jonathan nodded.

"Sorry I'm late," the other one said. "I got stuck in a traffic jam."

"Don't worry. I've got plenty of time."

11

Emily

It was eight o'clock in the evening and Emily was reading Stephen Hawking's "A Brief History of Time" when the doorbell rang. Emily didn't get up. It was probably a friend of her mother's. Mariella had disappeared hours ago into the sunroom, which she used as a studio, and was carving a stone. The bell rang again.

"At least answer it yourself!" Emily shouted.

"I can't stop now," her mother shouted back.

Emily stomped out of her room. "I'll call the police if this is Fred and you keep up the noise into the night."

She opened the door.

"Oh. Hi, Paula."

Her school bus driver was the last person she expected to see.

"Hello, Emily. You wanted to interview me, so I decided to come along on the off-chance. Or..." she looked uncertainly past Emily, "is it too late already?"

"No, not at all. Why?"

"Because your mother is already in her nightdress."

Emily turned round. Her mother had crept up, her face dusty, a chisel in her hand. To Emily she looked like a madwoman, ready to attack the unannounced visitor at any moment.

"It's just her artist's clothes," Emily said.

"And she hasn't slept since 2012."

"Funny." Emily's mother pushed past her daughter. "So you're the astronaut my daughter's crazy about? Come in, don't stand out in the cold."

She pulled Paula into the house and led her into the kitchen. When Emily had told her about the new driver, she had obviously been listening. Emily was surprised. Her mother usually seemed absent to her. And it got even better.

"Have you eaten yet?" Emily's mother asked. "I'll make a

quick snack. Let's see, where do we have ..."

"Baked beans are in the pantry," Emily said. "Assuming you haven't used the sauce for another painting."

"I work with natural materials," Emily's mother said to Paula. "Earth, flowers, food, whatever's available. But let's be on a first-name basis. My name is Mariella." Meanwhile, she had found some crackers in the cupboard and spread them with cream cheese.

"My name is Paula," said Paula. "But please don't bother, I've only come for the interview."

"And I'm so glad!"

Mariella lowered her voice. "Emily hardly has any friends at school. She thinks they're all superficial and not interested in her hobby. But please: Who likes maths? Emily doesn't like it herself, she's just trying to fill a niche where she can be special. A special outsider."

"I'll go and set the light for the recording," Emily said.

With a bang, she shut the door to the kitchen behind her. Another 1486 days until she turned 18 and could move out! Numbers were something to hold on to, even if they were big.

Emily usually drank a glass of apple juice before recording, but the juice was in the kitchen, with her mother. If she had to see her again today, Emily would smash dishes, and her mother would like that because it was impulsive and wild. It was impossible to be a normal teenager when your parents didn't care what nonsense you got up to, and good grades were seen as a sign of pitiful conformity.

"Space is infinite," Emily said to herself. "I'm sure there's intelligent life somewhere. I'm just on the wrong planet."

12

Paula

I ate a dozen crackers and turned down several offers to take part in artistic activities with Mariella. ("Have you ever worked with clay? It's liberating. Or how about expressive painting? Just throwing paint on a white piece of cardboard, anyone can do that. And may I draw you once in a while? You have that classic nose!")

As she poured herself a glass of wine, I finally managed to escape into Emily's room.

"Funny," I said. "Your mum didn't even want to know why I was wearing a bathing cap."

Emily waved it off. "You wouldn't think it was funny if you knew what kind of weirdos usually visit us."

She had mounted a camera on a tripod and turned her bed into a sofa with a blanket and cushions. Two glasses of water were placed on a stool. The scene was lit by two table lamps.

"What shall we talk about?" I asked.

"I've read that we owe a lot of technology to space travel. GPS, for example."

"Absolutely right," I said.

Why hadn't I read this before? I would have been better prepared. After all, I had been bored enough.

"But maybe it would be better if I started with something personal," I said.

"Yes, that sounds good."

I sat down on the sofa bed and folded my hands in my lap. Emily turned on the camera, gave me a thumbs up and sat down next to me.

"My maths lovers," she said, "I'm delighted to welcome a very special guest today: Paula, an aspiring astronaut."

"Hi." I waved at the camera.

But what could I say? Emily helped me start.

"Paula, we all know the Armstrong quote: One small step for man, one giant leap for mankind. When you think about how long astronauts train and how short a mission is in comparison - shouldn't it be: a few weeks in space, but half a lifetime to prepare? I mean, doesn't that sometimes seem tedious?"

"Good question, Emily. Of course it's hard sometimes. But you also learn things that are useful in everyday life."

"Really? Like what?"

"Mental strength. When you're on a space station, you can't just walk away if someone bothers you. You're forced to live with the other astronauts, their quirks and little annoyances. Once you've done that, nothing will get you down on Earth."

"But what if another astronaut is really mean? I imagine that would be difficult. How do you stay cool?"

"You can practise on Earth. How many people have siblings who are always better at everything? Or parents who are never happy with you?"

I winked at Emily. Her mouth curved into a smile.

Then we talked about astronaut food ("I just imagine it's a burger."), personal hygiene in zero gravity ("You have to catch drops of water and rub them on your skin.") and mess ("At home, dirty socks are left lying around. On the space station, they float in front of your nose.")

After half an hour, Emily brought the episode to a close and asked the viewers to write to her and tell her how much they had enjoyed the interview.

"This has been fun," she said as she switched off the camera. "Let's do it again."

"Let's see what the fans say."

"They'll love you."

"If you think. I'll see you in the morning."

"Five past seven. Get home safely."

In the hallway I bumped into Mariella. She must have been listening at the door.

"Are you leaving?" she asked. "Have a glass of wine with me."

"Thanks, but I have to drive."

"Emily said you are sleeping in the van."

"That's right."

"Great. I like that. I dream of reducing my possessions to one suitcase and leaving everything behind. Was it hard for you to let go?"

"Very much so." I thought longingly of my comfortable bed at home, where tourists now slept. "But you can hardly take anything on board a space shuttle."

"Leave your van with us tonight," Mariella said. "It's almost full moon, you should stay awake on such nights."

I didn't want to, but the prospect of a Wi-Fi connection and a bit of Netflix before bed was tempting. If I had to have a drink with Mariella, that was the price to pay.

She showed me into the sunroom, which she had converted into a studio. An electric heater kept the room comfortably warm despite the glass walls. It smelled of paint and solvents.

Mariella took a bottle of wine from a box of painting equipment, unscrewed it and poured it into water glasses for us. We settled into two rattan chairs and she began to talk about the paintings on the easels.

"Next I'm going to do something with tin," Mariella said. "To honour the work of you and your brave colleagues. Do you think the Space Agency would put that on display?"

I said I couldn't promise anything, but I could try to put in a good word for her.

"You are so inspiring!"

She toasted me. I raised my glass too.

I would never understand artists. What was all this talk about inspiration? Did they mean that in reality they did not have enough inspiration? Often I would have appreciated a little more order and quiet. It wasn't for fun that I used the blind shopping service. When I left my room, where every item was familiar to me, and entered a supermarket with shelves up to the ceiling, I was always overwhelmed by the choice. I would go in for cereal and come out with an overpriced unicorn-shaped nailbrush and rubber gardening boots ("Reduced! Only a few pairs left!").

I know that professionals are paid a lot of money to get you to spend, but it didn't help me to see through it. Still, I remained their victim.

In the end, the only option I could see was to use a blindfold to guide me through the oversupply. Whatever I discovered outside my shopping list, I had to ignore to avoid being exposed.

I was prepared for the supermarkets, but as I had painfully discovered, there were dangers outside the shops too.

After the first day of training with Jonathan, I felt exhilarated. I went home to tell my parents about my experience, but as usual they were less than enthusiastic. They asked about final exams, certificates and whether I had been promised a job.

I said they shouldn't be so petty and show more foresight. My mother replied that she and my father were very forward-thinking, that they were not born yesterday, and to prove it, they would use the fantastic possibilities of the Internet and offer my room on the Airbnb platform. The rent would go into a savings account for me, so I could buy potatoes and turnips in my old age, when I didn't get a pension.

I didn't want to spoil my good mood and went to my room (while I still could). But I was too excited to sit at the computer.

I had to get out and get rid of my excess energy. Aimlessly, I rode around on my bike, and eventually I ended up back in the hall where the astronaut training was taking place.

I leaned my bike against a street lamp and took a selfie. Maybe one day I would take journalists to this place and say: "This is where it all started: In a shed on the edge of town. But you don't need much in the beginning, just a dream and people who share it."

I wanted to take some more pictures inside, but the front door was locked. So I walked around the hall, found a window that could be pushed up and climbed in. My hand slipped over a sharp edge. When I turned on the flashlight on my mobile phone, I saw blood. It wasn't much, but I wanted to disinfect the wound just in case. I spotted a fully stocked first aid kit on a wall at the back of the hall and treated myself. As I put the roll of plasters back, I noticed the envelope. And then I saw the bills. Yes, I had opened the envelope, but who would suspect a hiding place among the plasters and gauze bandages? First aid kits say "Hello, here I am. Clearly visible and unlocked. Help yourself and take what you need."

I needed money. Not taking it would have seemed idiotic. So I put it in the inside pocket of my jacket, took a selfie of myself beaming with happiness and climbed back outside.

I want to emphasise that I had no criminal intentions. I knew the money was not for a big shopping spree or a short holiday. I hadn't even counted it so as not to let my imagination get the better of me.

My intention was to keep it safe and invest it in the astronaut programme when the opportunity arose.

I saw it as a test: the ground station couldn't dictate every step.

The astronauts had to act on their own responsibility, even if they had incomplete information ("Where did the money come from? How long has it been there?") This was my chance to prove myself. I would control myself and not spend the money on stupid things.

At first I succeeded. I went home, put the jacket with the money in it at the foot of my bed and went to sleep.

The next morning the telephone rang. It was Mrs Bunte. She said she had some bad news. It wasn't bad news. It was catastrophic news. The programme had been cancelled.

At first she was reluctant to say why, but when I pressed her, she said that the design had been a little too open, that the external expert had proved incompetent, and that when she had confronted him with this accusation, he had run off with part of the budget.

"Does that mean there will be no more swimming training?" I asked.

Yes, that's what it meant.

I was too depressed to say anything else. Mrs Bunte told me that she was very sorry and that I should come back today so that we could find an alternative for me.

I replied that I needed to collect myself first and hung up. Shortly afterwards Jonathan called me in his role as ground control. He played me two minutes of a film soundtrack.

"We can't take off right now because of a storm," he said.

"I understand," I said. "Let's hope the weather improves."

Then I played him "Fly me to the moon" in the Doris Day version. It was inappropriate, but I'd picked it out the day before and couldn't find anything else in a hurry.

After the last bars had died away, we fell silent. I don't think either of us knew whose turn it was. In radio communication, only one side can talk at a time, the other listens. Jonathan finally hung up.

I considered going back to bed and not getting up until Christmas. Jonathan had said that the rocket launch wasn't possible for the time being. Did that mean there was hope?

After all, we had made our wake-up call as planned.

What would an astronaut do in my situation? Certainly not sit around and do nothing. Besides, I was in danger of losing my home.

I got dressed, drove to the university, studied the flat-sharing notices on the notice board and wrote down a few telephone numbers.

But I wasn't in the mood for interviews where I'd say how much I liked cleaning bathrooms and kitchens. On the way back, I passed a used car dealership and spotted the van.

Yes, that's right, the van.

I just wanted to have a look at it, but these used car salesmen are even more cunning than supermarket decorators.

The salesman was young and he was flirting with me. Boss was out of town, so this was an opportunity for him to get me some good value. He could see how happy the car would make me.

I thought the price he gave me was really good. As I walked around the car, I counted the bills in the envelope and realized that I was only two hundred euros short. I negotiated the seller down by that amount.

"I'll pay in a minute, cash in hand."

It's something I've always wanted to say!

When I drove the van out onto the road, I felt invincible. Now I had both a car and a home. The seats of the van could be folded down into a bed, and thanks to the gas heating I wouldn't freeze. But after I had filled up with petrol, I realised why the car had been so cheap: it could only go in one direction.

The salesman had mentioned problems with reverse, but I thought that was a warning to shift carefully. Wrong.

I tried to look on the bright side. Now I didn't have to worry about tight parking spaces because I couldn't get into them. Instead, I pulled up in front of our house in the second row of the street, gathered some of my most important things and loaded them onto the van (ignoring my mother, who had come home for her lunch break and was watching the whole thing).

I felt a sense of satisfaction. She must have thought I would only give up my room if she threatened to evict me. Well, she was wrong. I was gone, on my way to the only acquaintance with enough room to turn around in front of his door: Roger.

It was only on the drive to his place, as the settlements along the country road grew sparser and even the cows began to stand around one by one, that it dawned on me what role I must have played in the end of the astronaut programme. It was I who had run off with part of the budget.

But what do you do when there's no reverse gear? I had to look forward.

That's what happens when I'm inspired.

13

Jonathan

Jonathan crouched on the cold tiles of a single changing room and watched the flip-flops of the swimmers passing by. His knees ached and he was becoming more familiar with the floor of this Munich pool than he would have liked. It desperately needed mopping. There were hairs, loose patches and clipped nails lying around.

Finally Jonathan saw Viv's neon yellow trainers.

"Hey," he whispered. "I'm in 213."

When he heard Viv stop, he unlocked the door. Viv squeezed into the cubicle, put her gym bag on the bench and gave him a big hug.

"Finally you're here!" she said.

"You took your time! I've been waiting here for fifteen minutes."

"Dad got off work late. I must hurry, the coach is waiting."

"Is this game of hide and seek really necessary? Why don't we just have a cup of tea somewhere after training?"

"No, I told you not to let the new coach or dad see you. Otherwise they'll think I'm up to something and then I won't be allowed to go to the cinema on Sunday. But it's my only ray of hope."

Viv kicked off her shoes and started to take off her jumper.

"Stop!" Jonathan shouted.

"I don't have time. We need to talk while I change."

"Wait, I'll go into the next cubicle."

"Nonsense. Just look away."

She pushed him into a corner of the cubicle and threw her towel over his head.

"That's a stupid idea," Jonathan muttered under the towel curtain. He was not happy. What if the lifeguard walked by and saw two pairs of legs in the cabin?

"I need to sit down and get my feet off the floor."

Viv led him to the bench and pushed him down by the

shoulders. She was strong.

How could she still fail to beat her personal bests? Jonathan had five minutes at most to find out.

"What was your training plan last week?" he asked.

Viv rattled off a list of routes and drills.

"That's only a slightly higher workload than I used to give you," Jonathan said. "If you've slowly increased the intensity of your training, your body should adapt."

"But the new coach makes me feel like I can't do it."

It would have been easy for Jonathan to agree with Viv and join her in railing against the coach, but he held back. A good astronaut puts the success of the mission before his own interests. Viv was about to enter the water, and if she didn't give it her all, she would fall further behind the competition.

"You need to get positive images in your head," Jonathan said. "Think about your last win. What did you feel during the race? What did you hear? What did it smell like in the hall?"

"It smelled like coffee and damp towels," Viv said. "But that was in Dortmund. Here, even the bathrobes smell of Chanel No. 5. I hate Munich. All this poshness makes me want to puke."

Jonathan heard the snap of elastic against bare skin and breathed a sigh of relief. Apparently Viv was properly dressed again.

"You can look now." She pulled the towel from his head. "Hey, is that flower for me?"

She bent down to pick up the plant that lay wrapped in paper on the floor.

"I almost forgot," Jonathan said. "It's a succulent. So you'll have something to take care of."

Put like that, it sounded strange. He would have to explain the idea behind the gift.

"I was hired as a coach for an astronaut programme," he said. "So I've been learning a lot about space travel lately. Do you know what the greatest psychological challenge is in orbit?"

"Loneliness," Viv said.

"That's right. Astronauts have different strategies for coping. Many write diaries, but some grow plants to distract themselves and feel less isolated. A French astronaut was the first to cultivate a flower in space. He also wrote a blog from the perspective of the courgette he was keeping in a plastic bag. The zucchini describes life on the space station. You should read it, it's funny."

"I don't have time to read."

"Yes, I know. That's why I brought you an easy-care plant. It only needs watering once a week. If its stems get too long, you can just cut them off."

Jonathan made a dismissive gesture with his hand. The plant idea had seemed good to him during the car ride. He had assumed that Viv would feel lonely after moving to a new school and a new team. But maybe that wasn't the case. Maybe Viv was a lone wolf and didn't miss anything - apart from athletic success. Jonathan was wasting her time with care advice for a desert plant.

"Vivian?" someone called from the corridor.

"I'd better be going," Viv said.

She carefully tucked the plant into an outer pocket of her gym bag.

"We have to somehow convince my parents to bring you here and fire the new guy, Jonarhan! We could say that your mental practise is better. The new guy does that too, but I could say my English isn't good enough to understand the things he wants me to do."

"Vivian!" shouted the other coach again.

"I'll think of a strategy," Jonathan said. "Call me back and don't screw it up."

"Bye, coach."

Viv winked at him, slipped out the door and was gone.

Jonathan put his feet on the ground. He could go home now. He had organised a ride for the evening. It would take all night. Ten minutes with Viv would have cost him sixteen hours travelling by car. But compared to travelling in space, that wasn't much, and travelling on Earth didn't expose you to cosmic radiation that made you age faster. On the contrary, Jonathan felt fresh and hopeful.

14

Emily

Emily was angry at her mother. This was not an unusual situation, but the reason was new. Suddenly Mariella was interested in Emily's hobby, and that was annoying.

After Mariella hadn't been allowed to attend the recording of the interview, she had apparently watched the final clip on the Internet. Emily had posted it that very same evening. A few hours later, her mother woke her up.

"Emily, you have to read this!"

Mariella approached Emily's bed with her laptop. The computer was ten years old and its fan was running at the noise level of a hairdryer.

"What?" Emily blinked. "It's only half past four."

"So?" Mariella asked. "I haven't slept yet."

"But I have!"

"Why? Is there anything important planned for tomorrow?"

"Just school, Mum."

"Well, you see. Now listen to what people write to you: 'Great interview.

A friend of mine sent me the link. I don't usually watch science channels, but the astronaut came across nice.' And another: 'I thought NASA only took people with straight A's. Then I might have a chance.' Oh, and this: 'Are you doing a second episode? Can we send you questions?'"

"You don't have to read me all the comments."

"My dear daughter, I'm impressed. Who would have thought that you would do something that so many people would like?"

The motherly pride was something Emily could have tolerated. But Mariella didn't want to be just a fan. When Emily entered the kitchen in the morning, the table was set.

"You've got fresh rolls?" Emily could hardly believe her eyes.

"For the three of us, so we can start the day comfortably. Or end it, whatever." Mariella laughed excitedly. "I haven't even been to bed yet. What do you think, is Paula up already?"

"As if you'd consider that. Just knock on her door and wake her up."

"Oh, oh. Someone's got a grudge."

"I'm tired!"

Mariella raised her hands as if she had nothing to do with the situation and disappeared to fetch her guest. Paula was surprised to be invited to breakfast, and even less expected the positive feedback from the people who had seen the interview.

"Wow," she said after Mariella had read out a selection of the comments. "I thought the video would be watched a few times and only a couple of Paula's fans would like it. But that they would all react so positively..."

"You've hit a nerve," Mariella said. "You're going to be a star, Paula."

"I hope not."

Now Paula looked startled.

Emily gave her mother a warning look.

"Thanks for the coffee and the roll." Paula stood up. "I have to put my bedding away in the van. The school run starts soon."

"Don't forget the wake-up call," Emily said.

Later she cursed herself for saying it. She had wanted to prove to her mother that she knew more about Paula's astronaut programme than she did, that she was privy to details that only experts would understand. But it backfired.

While Paula was on the phone, Mariella asked Emily questions. Emily gave Jonathan's name and said he was a swimming coach. It wasn't much, but it was enough for Mariella to get even more involved.

"I have a surprise for you," Mariella announced that evening. "Tomorrow we're going to do something nice together."

"So?" Emily opened the freezer and was delighted to see pizza inside. Her mother must have gone shopping. "Do you have another event planned? I won't clear my room for it. We've got a chemistry test next week and I need a quiet place to study."

"No party. But I thought we'd be hungry after sports. Hence the pizza."

"We're doing sports?"

"Oops, now I've given it away. We're having swimming lessons."

"Mum?!"

"With a really great coach."

"You booked Jonathan."

"Exactly, for both of us. We'll meet at the pool at half past nine. Paula can come with us and save herself the wake-up call. Or no, I have a better idea!" Mariella grabbed Emily's arm. "The two of them will make the call live and unplugged. For us."

"You think the whole world is just for your amusement, don't you?"

"What have I done wrong now? Jonathan is a top coach. An hour with him doesn't come cheap. And by the way, I know about your trip into town. I spoke to Nele. You were going to bring Jonathan yourself."

"But then I changed my mind. We shouldn't interfere. They don't want to meet at the moment. That makes sense. Four hundred kilometres separate them. That's how far the International Space Station is from Earth."

"Bollocks. I bring people together, that's my talent. Should Paula remain a school bus driver forever? Apart from the phone calls, she doesn't do anything spacey at the moment. But you'll need material for your next interview.

"Nobody wants to see you trying to learn to crawl."

"Then don't film me, film the coach. Do an interview with ground control."

"And if I don't want to?"

Why did her mother have to interfere in everything? Probably the only reason Mariella was happy about the comments under the video was because she saw an opportunity to be in the spotlight herself.

Emily took a family pack of ice cream from the freezer. She would have preferred something savoury, but if she stayed in the kitchen with her mother for another minute to unwrap the pizza and put it in the oven, she would go mad. The ice-cream was ready for consumption. Emily would eat stracciatella in her room until her stomach hurt, and her mother would be on the phone later, talking extra loudly to a friend, amused by the whims of teenagers.

Emily felt wetness on her foot. Condensation dripped onto her socks from the freezer door, which was still open. Emily had an idea. With a wicked smile she closed the door and said: "Oh, but the pool is closed. For repairs."

Mariella smiled back. "Sounds like I'll have to improvise. That's my favourite thing to do."

15
Paula

My van and I had moved in with Mariella and Emily.

"Because it saves me ten minutes in the morning," I had explained to Roger.

But he had guessed the real reason. "It's because of the internet. It's killing you all."

Now I parked in front of the garden fence that Mariella had built out of old cross-country skis. (She must have soon run out of material or desire, because the fence was only ten metres long).

The rent for my parking space was two euros a day. I was allowed to charge my laptop and phone from the socket in the garage and to take a shower in the house. Mariella had also promised to ask around the area if anyone needed a lift. I really liked my job now. There was never much traffic on the country roads in the area, I knew every single speed camera by now and the only challenge was not to fall asleep at the wheel.

When Mariella knocked on the door of the van on a Saturday morning, I thought someone needed a lift to the airport or the supermarket. But it was Mariella who needed me.

"I want to go swimming."

"But you have a car," I said.

"I can't drive, I've been smoking weed."

She pointed to her eyes. They looked normal. Anyway, I could use the extra income. So I told Mariella I would be happy to give her a lift.

"Emily's coming too."

The two of them would spend a mother-daughter morning together? I had a feeling it couldn't be true. But I wasn't expecting Jonathan.

He was sitting on the steps outside the pool and jumped up when he saw me. He obviously hadn't expected to see me either. The distance from where I'd parked the van to Jonathan was thirty metres, and because I couldn't stand the tension, I ran towards him. He ran towards me too, and when we reached each other, the only way to slow us down was to fall into each other's arms.

"What are you doing here?" he asked.

"I fly students to the school planet."

"Nice car. Do you live in it?"

I mumbled something about a temporary solution. Jonathan must have noticed the sudden change in my mood, but maybe he thought it was the stormy embrace. I hadn't yet told him that I'd only pretended to be autistic to get into the programme. But that little lie would probably be meaningless next to my theft.

Jonathan let me go. Mariella saved us from an awkward silence.

"So glad it worked out." She greeted Jonathan with kisses left and right. "I'm Mariella and this is Emily."

"And you both want to improve your technique?" Jonathan asked.

Mother and daughter shook their heads at the same time. They probably hadn't agreed on something like that in years.

"The pool's closed," Emily said. "Because of plumbing problems."

"Beautiful, the irony of fate." Mariella started to giggle, and when she saw our faces she burst into a fit of laughter that wouldn't stop. She was probably stoned after all. When she finally calmed down, she said: "But there's a lake nearby."

"It's April," I said.

"Of course I've got a wetsuit. I borrowed it from Sandra."

"But Sandra is a lot smaller than you," Emily objected.

"The wetsuit isn't for me anyway."

"You led me to the pool when you knew it was closed," I said. "And now you want someone to jump into the freezing lake in a wetsuit you've borrowed? But you two don't want to do it. And Jonathan is the coach. That just leaves me."

"I didn't know about the wetsuit," Emily said.

"That's even better. So you wanted me to catch pneumonia?"

Emily hunched her shoulders and looked crushed.

"I was just thinking about filming," she said. "It's foggy today, it'll be difficult."

"You want to put this training session on the internet too?"

Jonathan stood protectively beside me. "You don't have to take part in this nonsense, Paula. If I'd known what they were up to ..."

"I'm doing it," I said.

Why did I go along with this madness? I had a guilty conscience. I also had the ridiculous hope of being able to wipe out what I had done with a heroic act. So Jonathan could think: "This woman committed a theft for which I was accused and fired. Afterwards she acted as if everything was fine, but hey, then she went swimming outside in ten-degree weather, and that made a big impression on me".

We drove on, me with Mariella and Emily in front and Jonathan behind. I had expected a nice little pond with a sandy beach. But the lake was so big you wondered if you should walk around it to get to the other side or take the ferry. Only there was no ferry. Apart from some willow, there was nothing. We were standing in front of a lunar crater filled with ice-cold water.

"Has anyone ever swum in it?" I asked.

"My cousin took a dinghy in once," Emily said. "A rock sliced the boat open when she tried to pull it out of the water."

I can't say I was reassured by this information.

Mariella opened her bag.

"It's a neoprene dry suit," she said, "expensive stuff, keeps you warm."

"You could combine it with thermal underwear," Emily suggested.

But where would I get that?

The two of them got out of the car and I slipped back into my pyjamas. Getting into the dry suit was easier than I thought. Thanks to the bathing cap, I was already used to wearing tight clothing. I left the van in my flip-flops. Outside, Emily was setting up her camera.

"Is it OK if I film?" she asked.

I nodded. Whatever.

"Great, I'll broadcast live."

I walked over to Jonathan. "Looks like we have to deliver today," I said.

"Do you dare swim across the lake, Paula?"

"You're not serious! That's several kilometres."

"Nonsense. Maybe five hundred metres. That would be ten lanes in the pool. The suit will give you a bit of uplift."

"What I need is a propulsion," I said.

Jonathan ran his hand over his head and seemed to be thinking. I noticed his beautiful ears. They looked as if strong currents had pressed them against his skull.

"We don't have much opportunity for exercise today," Jonathan said. "I don't want you working with tools, the water's too murky for that. You wouldn't be able to see very well, and if something falls out of your hands, we probably won't be able to find it in the mud."

I swallowed. Would they find me if I went under? I was wearing a black suit and wouldn't be easy to see. After all, I was bigger than a screwdriver.

I heard Emily behind me: "Good morning, I hope many of you are awake and watching. Thank you for all the kind comments. Our astronaut Paula also appreciates your interest and has allowed me to join her for training today. It is important for astronauts to be in good physical condition. They prepare for their strenuous missions with endurance and strength training. Launching the rocket is not the hardest part. The acceleration generates forces of 3G, three times your body weight, but roller coasters generate up to 6G".

Amazed by these precise figures, I turned to see Emily reading on her phone.

"What is critical for their health is a prolonged stay in

weightlessness," Emily said. "Muscles and bone mass break down when they are not used as much. To counteract this, astronauts exercise several hours a day on treadmills and bicycles. If they didn't, they would be so weak on their return that gravity would kill them. They would collapse and die. So exercise is essential for survival. But let's ask Paula and her coach what's on the agenda for today."

She was getting Jonathan and me to stand in front of the camera.

"By swimming in the lake, we are simulating a moon walk," said Jonathan. "When astronauts land on an alien planet, they need to explore the environment. But at the same time they can't get too far away from the capsule. They must not run out of oxygen on the way back. The body uses more oxygen when it is moving than when it is resting. Paula will practise assessing her strength. Our goal is to swim across the lake, but today we will start with a partial distance. Paula will decide on the length herself".

"How are you doing Paula?" Emily asked.

"I'm excited," I said, "and even though I'm sweating, my feet are cold. That's weird."

"It'll be better in space," Jonathan said. "Spacesuits are heated. But let's get started before you freeze a toe."

"Good luck," Emily said.

Jonathan and I walked down to the shore. I put one foot in the water.

"With the temperatures, there should be ice on it," I said.

"It won't get any worse. The rest of your body will stay warm thanks to the suit. And as soon as you start moving, your blood will circulate faster and you'll feel strong."

"Do you really think I can swim to the other side?"
"Sure!"

I took a deep breath. I was no longer thinking about what had happened in the pool when I had tried to get the last screw out of the board. This was a completely different situation, I just had to swim straight ahead, one stroke at a time, simple movements that I had mastered since I passed my swimming badge at the age of six. Would it be fun? Probably not. But being an astronaut wasn't always all fun and games. Food came in pill form and on longer flights you wore diapers.

I slipped out of my flip-flops. I would have loved to do an elegant headfirst dive into the water for the camera, but it wasn't possible because the bottom of the lake was only slightly sloping.

Instead, I slowly stepped across the slippery ground into deeper water. I could feel sticky things on the soles of my feet and stones between them. Plants coiled around my legs. I couldn't feel them through my suit, but when I looked down I saw them. When I finally reached an area where I could swim, I got them between my fingers. It was disgusting. I didn't want that on my face. So I desperately held my head up and gave up underwater pulling and gliding. That slowed me down.

Gradually the plants in the water seemed to be getting less. Or had they grown so deep that they could no longer reach me?

... we probably won't be able to find it in the mud.

I looked back. Jonathan seemed far away now, but the opposite bank didn't seem to have got any closer.

Didn't distances appear shorter in the water? So in reality the two rescue points were even further apart. Soon I would have to decide whether to turn back or swim through. It was only then that I realised how isolated astronauts really were in space. They could communicate with the ground station, but what use was that in an emergency? They were beyond the reach of any help.

I would swim back! What was the point of getting it right the first time? Immediate success would only deprive me of the reason for training with Jonathan. We bonded over swimming and that was all we talked about. I couldn't even answer why I was living in the country without lying. My recent past had been inaccessible terrain, marshy as the bottom of a lake.

I took one last pull and turned around. My legs touched something. Frightened, I started to tip. I dipped one ear into the water and now the thing was on my hand too. Its surface was smooth. A whale? Moby Dick had found me! Scenes from the movie flashed through my mind. But then I felt the water plants again, and now I was glad they were there. Plants didn't grow on animals.

I pulled both knees to my chest, regained my balance, stretched my legs out and reached the ground. I was standing. The whale was a rock.

As soon as I straightened up, I knew I had made a mistake. Now I was only up to my knees in water and to go deeper into this hostile element seemed like madness. Mist hung over the water, blurring the contours of things.

"Enough rest," Jonathan shouted. "Keep swimming or you'll get cold."

But I couldn't. The water's surface shimmered darkly. There might be horrors lurking down there of which I had no idea. The undulating mirror could hide poisonous creepers, predatory fish or shipwrecks with razor-sharp metal edges.

"Come back, Paula!"

Jonathan's voice sounded different. Later I understood that the fog had muffled it, but at that moment on the rock, the figures on the far shore became a mirage with which the murderous lake tried to lure me.

"You've only been gone four minutes," Emily called. "You'll be back sooner than that."

"Pretend it was a desert," Mariella shouted.

Eventually all three of them shouted at me. But nothing could convince me. You may manage to jump into the freezing cold shower, but once you've escaped, nothing will get you back in. You know what it's like. Courage means ignoring what is awaiting you.

In the end, Jonathan saved me again. He stripped down to his underwear and crawled over to me. I think it only took him half a minute. Then he was standing on the rock too.

"Hold on to my shoulders and make yourself as stiff as a board," he said. "Can you do that?"

"I think so," I said.

The ground station gave instructions. This was good. I wasn't alone in space.

Gliding through the water behind Jonathan was both beautiful and terrifying. His presence calmed me. The muscles in his shoulders moved under my hands. But I also realised what a poor swimmer I was. My achievement had been not to drown. Even with me weighing him down, Jonathan could swim three times as fast. But at some point he started to sink.

"That's not funny," I shouted. "Stop it."

But Jonathan was going under. He disappeared into unreachable depths, leaving me alone. The predatory fish had taken him. In my fear, I must have kicked at the water to keep myself afloat. I remember screaming.

Suddenly my right arm was twisted behind my back. Jonathan had come up behind me. He held my arm with one hand and grabbed under my chin with the other. He turned me onto my back and pulled me towards the shore. Since he could only swim with his legs, we didn't make much progress.

"That hurts," I shouted. "You're twisting my wrist."

But instead of letting go, he squeezed harder.

I tried to reach Jonathan with my free arm, but I couldn't because he was pushing me away. So I used some of my breath to shout insults at him.

Finally Jonathan gave up and let me go. I felt mud on my shoulders. The astronauts were back on Earth, battered but alive. The press greeted them with towels.

16

Jonathan

Jonathan and Paula had to take Emily and Mariella home. Mariella insisted on heating up a can of chicken soup for the two of them. They sat in the kitchen, hunched over cups of hot tea, waiting for the microwave to go "bing".

"Do you mind if I take a picture of you?" Emily asked.

"Just one," Paula said. "You've really collected enough material today."

"That wasn't a moment of glory," Mariella said. "Wouldn't you rather delete your video, Emily?"

"I was broadcasting live. Once something is on the internet, anyone can copy it. Even if I took my version offline..."

Paula shrugged. "When the Challenger exploded, the whole world was watching. But ask Jonathan. It wasn't good publicity for him."

"Excuse me?" Jonathan straightened up. "I jumped into that freezing lake - without a dry suit - and brought you back before you caught pneumonia."

"But there's a gentler way! First you dived away to scare me, and then you almost dislocated my arm."

"You pushed me under and used me like a buoy. I only dived so that you would let go. Otherwise we would have both drowned. And the arm twist was necessary to keep you still. I didn't have all day. How long would I have lasted without insulating clothing? A few minutes at most."

"I'm sorry," Paula said meekly. "I didn't mean it. Didn't even realise what I was doing."

"That's all right. When you're scared, it's a normal reflex to cling to anything that holds you. I was a lifeguard at the Baltic Sea for a couple of summers and I'm used to a lot of things. But no one has ever cursed me as badly as you have. Even the drunks usually thank you when you fish them out of the waves."

"500 views already," Emily said. "And 32 new followers."

"At least one of them got something out of our stupid stunt," Paula said.

The microwave sounded. Mariella took out the bowl and poured steaming soup onto plates.

"Things don't always go smoothly," she said. "Now, more than ever, you should keep going. Fight, Paula! People want to see you try hard and eventually make it. That's what movies are all about. I'll ask Sandra if we can borrow the dry suit for a while, OK?"

Paula remained silent, staring into her plate as if expecting the bubbles of fat in the soup to form a message.

Emily broke the silence with another success story. "132 retweets on Twitter."

After lunch, Jonathan had to go to Mariella's studio and sit as a model. ("Just one sketch, it'll be quick. Your head shape is unique, you know that?") Only then could he say goodbye. He left the house with Paula.

They stood in front of their cars and started talking at the same time.

"Well..." Jonathan said.

"Sorry again ..." Paula said.

Jonathan grinned. "You first."

"You must think we've got some kind of nasty joke planned," Paula said. "First Mariella lures you here with a lie ..."

"You mean because she didn't want to swim herself? But she paid me."

"Then I go nuts..."

"It's not your fault."

"Maybe someone like me shouldn't do such things."

"Someone like you?"

"I'm scared."

"I've noticed that."

"I mean, sometimes I'm just so scared."

"Of what?"

"That's just it. Of nothing. I could be lying in bed and suddenly my heart starts racing, I'm sweating and I'm afraid I'm going mad."

"Can you do anything about it?"

"I could take medication. But everything that is out there has side effects. I guess I'll just have to learn to live with it. I've spent most of the last few years at home. I thought that if everything was always the same, things would get better. Unfortunately, that hasn't been the case. Paula waved her hand. "But enough about my condition."

"If you want me to coach you, I need to know. Are you afraid right now?"

"No. Why?"

"You said you didn't need a reason."

"That's true. But the last two situations in which I have been afraid have been really dangerous ones. That's confusing, but in a way it's good. If I'm going to be scared, I'd rather do something I can be proud of afterwards."

"But you don't want to start skydiving or free climbing now? I can't save you from the air."

"Swimming is fine for me. And I didn't get stranded on the rock on purpose. I just wanted to turn around, but then there was the rock and I got scared and suddenly I couldn't do anything."

"You took on too much. You have to learn when to listen to your fear because you've reached your limit. Only then can you go a little further each time. But just a little bit."

"How long do you think it would take me to swim across the lake?"

"Hard to say. You could probably do it in the pool. But there you could always take a break. In the lake, no. Every metre you swim further in, the way back gets longer. When you're in the middle, you have to keep going. It's important to remain calm. Your fear is draining your energy. You have to take long, economical strokes and manage your strength.

"You could come with me. Or I could do a swim along the

shore."

"But it's not the same. Ground control can only help from a distance. The astronaut has to do it alone."

"Do you even want to coach me after your experience today?"

"I'm not that easy to put off. Besides, Emily's fans would probably bombard me with nasty emails if I let you down."

"It's weird that people are watching me swim, isn't it?"

"I don't think so. There are more boring things on the web."

"So we're going on, coach?"

"I'm in if you are."

"Except I can't pay you, unfortunately."

"Then I'll just consider it free advertising. But I do have one question. Do you ever take your bathing cap off?"

"Only to sleep."

Paula blushed. Her expression became a little dismissive.

"But... are you all right?" Jonathan asked.

"I don't have cancer, if that's what you're getting at. I'm just bald. My hair bothered me, I cut it and it looked so stupid, so I shaved my head."

"I see." Jonathan tried to find a humorous way out, but came up empty. Paula had taken a step back and was playing with her car keys.

"I'm bald too," Jonathan finally said.

"But on me it looks like rubbish!"

Jonathan would have liked to contradict Paula and tell her how beautiful he thought she was, but that seemed inappropriate. Right now he was Paula's coach. He didn't mix business with romance, that only caused difficulties and in the end you got neither success nor love.

Jonathan would help Paula swim across this lake and then they could stop being astronauts and ground control and overcome the distance between them and ...

"We'll talk on the phone, right?" Paula said

"Wake up call at the usual time."

"I hope you haven't caught a cold today."

"Don't worry, I'll train for two hours and then go to the sauna."

He got into his car, waved out the window, started the engine and saw Paula getting smaller in the rear-view mirror.

She had to get through that lake. Jonathan had said that the training was free publicity for him, but Paula had no idea what was behind that line.

Jonathan pulled into the first rest area on the motorway, took out his phone and sent Viv the link to today's video. Below it he wrote: "Paula before mental training".

As soon as he'd sent it, he deleted it from his chat history so he wouldn't have to see it again. He felt shabby. He didn't have to wait long for a reply.

"Mum says if you can turn Paula into a fearless swimmer, she'll consider you again," Viv wrote back.

"The bet's on?" Jonathan wrote.

He waited anxiously for the reply.

"It's on," Viv wrote.

17

Emily

It was half past one in the afternoon when Paula finally pulled into the driveway. Emily was waiting.

"Tour's over, end of work for me," Paula said to Emily. "And you? Got a lot of homework today?"

"All done during the break," Emily said. "We still have plans for today."

"You could say that."

"Are you feeling fit?"

"I'm fine."

"You need a boost before training. Eat with us."

They went into the house. In the kitchen they found Mariella trying to make a coffee filter out of toilet paper.

"I have to go shopping again," she muttered. "Hi Paula, I was just about to cook something. What do you fancy?"

"That's OK, Mum," Emily said. "I'm making pasta. We don't have much time as we're going back to the lake soon."

She filled a pot with water and put it on the stove. While she waited for it to boil, she checked her emails on her phone.

"Two people from school are asking if they can watch the training live. And I have a message from a Dutch university. They're inviting you to try out their Soyuz simulator, Paula."

"Soyuz?" Mariella asked.

"That's a spaceship. They say they've recreated the capsule and the cockpit so that students can practise flying it. Wouldn't that be cool? There are photos of it online."

Paula looked over Emily's shoulder.

"Looks complicated."

"How did the university find out about you?" Mariella asked.

"They've seen our videos," Emily said. "Apparently we're already internationally famous."

Mariella opened the fridge. "Oh, shoot. We're out of parmesan."

She could be happy for us, Emily thought. Instead she's offended that for once she's not the centre of attention. She was just a spectator at swimming practice, and now she feels left out, and the nice comments on our videos no longer interest her. She won't mention them again until there's a nasty remark. But I'm curious to hear what she has to say about Ruben. She won't be able to ignore *him*.

They heard the moped just as they'd finished eating. Mariella craned her neck to look out of the kitchen window.

"That guy's coming towards us. Who is he?"

"Just a friend," Emily said casually. "His name is Ruben, but who cares, he's just another weird outsider. I know him from the chess club. He was county champion last year. But of course he only plays to be interesting. Nothing like that is fun."

She stifled a grin. Paula looked between her and Mariella.

"When he rides a motorbike ..." Mariella said.

"Yes, he turned 16 last month," Emily said. "But he hasn't celebrated yet. If he invites me, can I go to his party?"

Ruben parked his motorbike in front of the garden fence and took off his helmet. He brushed his shoulder-length hair behind his ears and polished his glasses on the corner of his hoodie. As he put them back on, he looked over at the house, where all three women were now standing at the window. Ruben waved. Emily's heart melted a little.

"I'll open the door for him!"

A little later, Ruben was sitting at the table with them, scooping up ice cream - the one food Mariella never forgot to buy.

"Do you like it?" Mariella asked. "Or would you like some topping on it? I think we have sprinkles."

Emily rolled her eyes.

"Sprinkles? Mum! We're not twelve anymore."

"You weren't that long ago, little lady. So tell me, Ruben, you're a chess champion?"

"No, I just play for fun. But your daughter is very good.

She's already beaten me twice. Do you play too? Have you taught her all the openings? Emily starts each game differently. She's inscrutable."

Paula nudged Emily and winked at her. Emily bit down on her spoon, hoping no one could tell how flattered she was.

Meanwhile, Ruben seemed to realise how little Mariella could relate to chess and changed the subject.

"I'm also a member of the Chaos Computer Club. For some time now, people there have been planning to launch their own satellites so that we can set up an independent communications network. And if they succeed, I'm sure a hacker will go into space one day."

Mariella seemed impressed. "Just normal people? That's possible?"

"Hackers aren't normal people. I'm joking. And yes, it is possible. Of course, you still need a lot of money, not only for the technology, but also to pay experts to work full-time on the project. Crowdfunding is one way. We need attention so that people decide to support us with small or large amounts. And for that we need vloggers like Emily to get others excited about space travel. She has already inspired me." He turned to Paula. "But I haven't asked yet: do you mind if I come with you to the lake today?"

"Sure," Paula said. "We should start charging admission. Has anyone looked at the clock? We've got to get going."

"Go on, I'll tidy up."

Mariella smiled angelically, but Emily didn't trust her mother. Mariella usually managed to turn the conversation to her art. This time she hadn't tried. Had the mother-daughter rivalry between them been suspended? Not at all.

"Don't forget your retainers, Emily," Mariella said. "The dentist said to wear them during the day."

18
Paula

When we reached the lake I was still confident. Today I would swim to the rock, rest if necessary and then turn back. I would make it back to shore on my own. It wasn't far, I could have done it in the pool. It was all mental. My performance would strengthen me inside and next time I would make it past the rock. Eventually I would manage to swim the whole lake.

The night before I'd googled "fear of natural water" and found out that I wasn't the only one with this problem. There's even a name for it: thalassophobia.

While Emily set up her camera and explained to Ruben what she was shooting, I changed into my dry suit in the van.

"You're warm and rested," I said to myself. "Ready for the countdown."

Jonathan was waiting outside.

"You ought to have a go at surfing," he said. "You've already got the right car for it."

He pointed to a bumper sticker on the door that said "I love Hawaii".

The way Jonathan looked at my van made me uncomfortable. What if he remembered seeing it at the dealership? I still had no idea how I was going to make up for my theft and the consequences for Jonathan. With the money I made driving school buses, I'd have to save for years to come up with enough.

My guilt grew as Jonathan put more and more time into our astronaut project. Completely unselfishly, he spent his time training with me instead of coaching better swimmers.

The only way I could return the favour was to make an effort and give Emily good pictures. If Jonathan and I had positive experiences together and hopefully became a couple, the stupid van thing would become irrelevant. Maybe Jonathan would catch the eye of important people with the help of Emily's videos. Maybe he would even become the psychological coach for the national soccer team.

I was making fantastic plans for the future. Honesty was not an issue in them. My plan was never to admit what I had done. Little did I know how many people had already noticed Jonathan.

After Emily told me the equipment was ready, I jogged along the shore for a minute to warm up my muscles and conferred with Jonathan.

He said: "Don't stop. Turn around if you have to, but keep moving. If you think you're going to get scared, turn that fear into energy."

I gave him the thumbs up sign, swung my arms and waded into the water. As soon as it was above my waist, I swam away.

Behind me I heard Emily say: "Astronauts usually work as a team, but there are times when they are completely on their own, for example when they leave the space station to repair something. Although they are usually in radio contact with their colleagues, they have to rely on their own skills if radio contact is lost for any reason. A few years ago there was an incident that almost cost a crew member his life. During an external mission, the astronaut noticed water seeping into his helmet. It was probably coming from his drinking bag. The radio link was lost and the level of liquid in the helmet rose above the astronaut's mouth, nose and finally his eyes. He could not breathe and could barely see. With the last of his strength he groped his way back to the airlock. Why am I telling you this? Haven't we all been afraid of the dark? Now imagine being in a place no human has ever been before, in cold, dark space, alone in zero gravity..."

Her voice faded the further I swam. I turned round. Ruben's presence seemed to have awakened a poetic side in Emily. Or maybe Emily was so excited because another spectator had joined us. But why was she talking to Jonathan? I jumped and thought I'd been caught in a cold current. But it was just fright. The person standing on the bank was Mrs Bunte.

What was she doing here? Had I been caught? Had cameras recorded my theft and now I was to be arrested? If so, any attempt to escape was futile. By the time I reached another part of the shore, the police would be there. But I didn't see anyone in uniform. Mrs Bunte seemed to have come alone.

I turned and swam back to shore. If someone had told me beforehand that I was going to sweat while swimming on a spring day, I'd have thought them stupid. But now I realised it was possible. When Jonathan spotted me on the way back, he went to where I had taken off my flip-flops and held them out to me. I think he was trying to get away from Mrs Bunte, but she followed him and talked to him. Apparently she had entered the video because Emily was waving frantically. Mrs Bunte didn't react and Ruben finally had to pull her away by the arm.

Water had got into my ears and I couldn't understand what they were saying. As my knee touched the ground and I stood up, the conversation stopped and gave way to a reverent silence. I waded to shore, feeling foolish. What great thing had I done? But as Emily was still filming and gesturing to me, I slipped into my flip-flops and shuffled over to her.

"Paula," she said, "how was it today? You didn't swim as far as last time, did you have any problems?"

"I had problems with the equipment," I said. "The water must have got warmer. I was sweating."

To emphasise my words, I wiped my wet forehead. Feeling I needed to give the crowd a little more drama, I added: "And then I got a cramp in my calf. That's why I stopped early and turned back."

"Perhaps you lack magnesium," Emily said.

"That's possible. I'll talk to the trainer about my diet."

Emily took that as a signal to stop and began her dismount. When she had switched off the camera, Mrs Bunte rushed towards me. She greeted me with a firm handshake.

"Good to see you again, but why are you hiding here? I only found the lake because my grandparents lived nearby and

I know the area well."

"Give Paula five minutes," Jonathan said. "She has to change first."

I disappeared into the van and hurried so Jonathan wouldn't be left alone with Mrs Bunte. He had seemed upset and tense.

A little later I understood why. Mrs Bunte had seen Emily's videos and thought we were continuing the astronaut training programme on our own.

"But we don't need to hire students for media work," she said. "We have professionals for that. Our press officer can put you in touch with the relevant media."

Emily crossed her arms in indignation and started to interject, but Jonathan cut her off. "I've already told you: we don't want anything more to do with your organisation. And I certainly don't want to work with you personally. I've lost my swimming groups because of you."

"Which was your own fault. Someone who embezzles public money is no longer acceptable."

"I didn't take a single euro. But since you don't believe me, I'm beginning to regret it.

"So you admit that you had access to the budget."

"As I said, Mr Keunecke tried to give it to me. When I didn't take it, he left it in the hall."

"As far as that goes, it matches Mr Keunecke's account. But Mr Keunecke claims that no one else knew where the money was. Only you could have taken it."

"Then why don't I hide? But Mr Keunecke is still missing, isn't he? You can't get hold of him at his shop. They say he's on a business trip."

"Probably in the Bahamas," I said.

Mrs Bunte pointed at me. "I think it was like this: the three of you wanted to share the money, but then Mr Keunecke ran off with it all by himself."

"Don't blame Paula too," said Jonathan.

He was so chivalrous! I felt worse and worse. Jonathan was

getting into it now.

"You should work on your attitude. How do you expect to help people if you think everyone is a potential criminal?"

"I don't," Mrs Bunte said. "When I saw the videos, I actually thought they might be a solution to please all sides."

"I don't understand."

"So far I've refrained from calling the police. Firstly, I don't have any hope of them finding the money, and secondly, the matter would become public and we wouldn't look good. Mr Keunecke gained our trust and deceived us. He is not an expert on European funding initiatives, nor is he in any way qualified in the field of training - except perhaps in training car salesmen. Let's face it: the money is gone. But it wasn't supposed to be in our bank account anyway. We were supposed to use it to prepare people to be astronauts".

"I think I know what you're getting at," I said. "Jonathan and I should act as if our training is funded."

"Exactly."

"But it isn't," Jonathan said. "And what about the other participants? Do they still have to polish their CVs every day? Autistic people have a hard enough time on the job market."

Mrs Bunte looked embarrassed. "We had difficulties filling all the places in the programme before, so we didn't look too closely at the participants. Now we're offering a programming course, and the applicants there seem to me to be much more ... eh ... autistic." She looked at me apologetically. "Was that offensive?"

I waved her off generously.

"I'll summarise," Jonathan said. "You hired me for a dubious programme. After I refused to take money from Mr Keunecke, you accused me of stealing it. I lost my swimming lessons. And in return, they want me to work unpaid to make it look like the budget was well spent."

"The false accusation is your version of things. Let's stick to the facts. Mr Keunecke was an old acquaintance of yours. You don't deny that, do you?"

"I went to school with him. I can't help it."

I put a hand on Jonathan's arm to calm him down. "We're training anyway. Let her support us."

"I'd love to," Mrs Bunte said.

"What do you have in mind?" Jonathan asked. "Do you have a Soyuz simulator in the basement? If you want to help, give me back my swimming groups. I'd also like the lifeguard duties back during the school holidays. You know, I like being around people in swimwear. Because they don't have pockets to hide money in."

His mobile phone rang.

"We can talk about absolutely anything," Mrs Bunte said.

"Just a moment." Jonathan took the call and moved a few metres away.

"Not again..." I heard him say. "Stay calm. Are you feeling dizzy? Eat something sweet. Have a glass of water ... Have you checked your bed? I'll be right there."

He hung up and came back to us.

"Unfortunately I have to go. My father needs me."

"I'll come with you," I said.

"To my father?" Jonathan seemed surprised.

"Yes, we haven't met yet."

Please don't leave me with Mrs Bunte, I tried to say with a look. Jonathan seemed to understand.

"If you like. Follow me."

"But I have to take Emily and Ruben home first."

"I can do that," Mrs Bunte said. "My car is parked down the road. Where do you have to go?"

Emily explained.

When the three had left, Jonathan said: "She must be serious about making herself useful. Good, she won't bother us that way. You're free for the rest of the day."

"Aren't you going to introduce me to your father?"

"I thought that was just an excuse to get rid of Mrs Bunte."

"Wrong."

It was Saturday lunchtime and I had a day and a half ahead

of me with no plans. I wanted to ask Jonathan if he wanted to go to the cinema that evening, but I was afraid he'd say no. Did he like me? I thought he did. But he was still cold. I guess he just took the astronaut programme too seriously. Love affairs between crew members are not encouraged. I'd heard of two American astronauts who had been in a relationship before a mission, so NASA only assigned them to shifts that didn't overlap. While one worked, the other slept.

But a parental visit was harmless. Why did Jonathan hesitate?

"All right, I'll take you," he said. "But I'm warning you: My dad's place isn't tidy."

As I followed Jonathan's car into town, I pictured a dingy one-bedroom flat with piles of dishes in the sink, dirty laundry in the corners and withered plants by the window. The block was a seventies housing estate. Jonathan unlocked the front door.

"The lift is broken," he said.

We went up to the fourth floor and Jonathan rang the doorbell of a flat at the end of the corridor.

"I've got a visitor," he shouted.

He said to me: "Let him open the door himself and he'll be dressed."

The handle was pushed down and I heard a grinding sound as the door opened a crack. Someone on the other side was breathing heavily. Jonathan's father seemed to be struggling.

"This is as far as it goes," he said.

"Get out of the way, I'll push against it," Jonathan said.

He waited a moment, then threw himself against the door. Plastic cracked.

"Watch out for the marble run," Jonathan's father shouted.

Now we could get in.

The flat was a jungle, impenetrable off the beaten track. There were things lying around. Lots of things. They were wedged together and leaned against each other. Small things were under big things, soft things hung over square things, and flexible things were stuffed into spaces.

But after the initial shock, I began to see patterns in the apparent chaos. Next to a box of women's boots was shoe polish, followed by a collection of umbrellas, plastic bags, a honey jar filled with tokens for shopping carts, bonus stamps, returnable bottles, cups with different brands of beer printed on them, a pink plush bear like the ones you win at shooting ranges, part of a neon sign and a bar stool with a tattered cover. Each thing seemed to have a connection to its neighbour, as if Jonathan Vater had started a puzzle that no human could complete.

I had spent a lot of time in rooms myself and knew how they could hypnotise you. It happens slowly, and you only notice it when you're lying on the bed and can't move an object. Everything seems to be immovably in its place. Making a mess is different from tidying up. When things are freed from their packaging, they gain strength and seem to solidify, like plasticine that dries in the air and becomes rock hard.

Ordinary mortals could not master this apartment, it needed a fiercely determined tidying crew, men and women whose hearts would not be softened by melancholy stuffed animals and sentimental mementos. Or a fire, that would do too.

Jonathan introduced me to his dad.

"Pleased to meet you, Mr Meine," I said. "Your son has saved me from drowning twice. Did he tell you that?"

"No, I haven't," Jonathan said. "And I'm afraid there's no time for a chat over coffee now. We're looking for a tin of heart medication, something about this big." He measured the height of a shot glass with his fingers. "And it could be anywhere, right, Dad?"

"No. I haven't been in the kitchen since yesterday morning," Mr Meine said. "We can rule that room out."

"You're killing me," Jonathan said.

I smiled as nicely as I could. The old man was obviously

embarrassed to have me around. When was the last time he had a strange person come to visit him? But now I was here, I had already seen the corridor and I might as well stay and help find the medicine.

I entered the first room. I couldn't tell what function it might have had. In one corner there was a huge television set on a wobbly pedestal made of picture books, but I had already seen two other cathode ray tubes in the corridor. So it didn't necessarily mean I was in the living room.

I could hear Jonathan and his father talking in the corridor.

"A marble run," Jonathan said. "What kids are going to play with it?"

"You could have told me." Mr Meine sounded reproachful. "I wasn't prepared for visitors."

"Oh! And if I had told Paula, would the place have been tidy?"

"Don't talk to me like that."

"I would have vacuumed for a young lady. I can still do a quick ..."

"Paula doesn't mind the dust. She's going to be an astronaut. If she can find your medicine in this hostile environment, she'll have no problem finding water on Mars. Come on, you'd better look with me. Let's go through the bedroom.

They went next door.

Dust, I thought, that might help me.

The flat didn't smell. Mr Meine didn't seem to be the sort of messy person who left food on the floor and didn't take out the rubbish. Even the worn-out mountain bike tyres hanging from a coat rack seemed to have been cleaned before. Still there was dust everywhere. It was getting thinner towards windows and thicker deeper indoors. In the light of the midday sun, I could see exactly which objects had been used recently. A paperback book with gold lettering on the cover shone as if it had just been polished. Mr Meine must have read it recently. That's right, a shopping list with yesterday's date stuck between the pages as a bookmark.

Detective work was called for. What other utensils could Mr Meine have used while reading? If you sat still, you would get cold. But a hot-water bottle sandwiched between two originally packaged filter coffee machines didn't hide the medicine. I spotted a neatly folded cardigan that seemed to be floating on a lake of sailing calendars. I had to climb on one knee onto a high chair to reach the jacket, but I was disappointed again. None of the pockets contained the medication. Apparently it wasn't that simple. I had to think outside the box.

Book - park bench - rainy weather - shoe polish? No, nothing here either.

Book - suspense - funny part - telephone? But I didn't see the telephone.

Book - biscuit - crumbs - lint roll?

The lint roll was only halfway into its case. I pulled it out and found what I was looking for. The lint roll wrapper had the right diameter for the pill box. There it was!

"Mr Meine!"

He came in, Jonathan in tow, and wouldn't stop thanking me. I was modest, but I think I gained a few inches. I may have been afraid of subterranean life in swimming lakes, but I was good at detective work.

"How can I show my appreciation?" Mr Meine asked.

I raised my hands defensively. I didn't want a reward! But then I had an idea.

"You have some extraordinary things here," I said.

Behind his father's back, Jonathan clapped his hands over his head and made a desperate face.

I didn't let him put me off.

"I saw some windows and metal parts on the balcony," I said. "Do you still need them?"

"That used to be a greenhouse," said Mr. Meine.

"I'd like to donate it to a school." I said to Jonathan: "Emily has project days next week. Let's ask Mariella to build a research station with some of the pupils using the greenhouse material. It doesn't have to look realistic, they should just have fun being artistic. This would not only give Mariella a task, but we could also send Mrs Bunte to her. Pupils, art, technology and the future - those are the keywords she needs for her public relations work."

Jonathan rubbed his chin. "My father could write us a bill for the materials. We can use it to justify why the budget has already been spent. But Emily won't be happy at all if you put her mother in touch with the school."

"I don't think she cares. She will be teaching chess and will only see her mother during the break. Knowing Mariella, she'll plunge headlong into work until the janitor kicks her out at night. That'll give us a break from her."

"And Emily too."

"Yes, especially Emily. They don't get on at all. Their characters are completely opposite. We should separate them to avoid arguments within the crew."

"You're already thinking like a real astronaut."

"Aren't I?"

We loaded the greenhouse parts into my van.

Mr Meine had even found some packing blankets in his jungle, which we used to wrap the glass.

"That's it," Jonathan said as we closed the back doors of the van.

"Everything's inside. Drive carefully."

My heart sank. I hadn't expected a kiss, but "drive carefully" was a bit meagre for a goodbye. Our relationship seemed to be cooling. But there was no time to waste. Our existence on Earth is the blink of an eye compared to everything else. Scientists had discovered that the universe was already 80 million years older than previously thought. What a number. If all those years could be overlooked, what was the duration of a human life compared to that? And there was so much emptiness around us. I wanted to hold on to Jonathan so we wouldn't drift apart again. But he was so smooth. There was nothing to hold onto.

"Look after your father," I said. "He's not eating enough."

"How can you tell?"

"Because the last time he was in the kitchen was yesterday morning."

Jonathan seemed to be thinking. I took advantage of his uncertainty and went back into the house.

"I'll fix him something quickly."

19

Jonathan

"Your girlfriend's a real gem."

Jonathan's dad ran his hands over his stomach and looked down with satisfaction at the Tupperware bowl containing the remains of the stew Paula had conjured up from what was left in the fridge.

"She's not my girlfriend," Jonathan said.

"Anyway, she can cook."

"So can I."

"But you don't like to. Paula does."

"Probably because she doesn't get the chance. She lives on a van and there's no room to prepare anything elaborate." Jonathan looked around scowling. "Not here either, though."

"Don't pick on me."

"You have to change something. The flat is no longer safe. Think what would happen if there was a fire."

"I just find it so hard to get rid of stuff. You can still use a lot of these things. We saw that again today."

"Are you talking about the greenhouse parts? Paula could have got them from a scrap yard."

"But then they would have cost money. I rescued them from the rubbish and Paula saw them. She found them suitable for her purposes and took them. That's the way to do it. You take what's there, especially if it's pretty. Heed this advice, my son."

"Dad! I'll pretend I don't understand. Anyway, I have to go to training now."

"I think you'd make a wonderful couple. What bothers you about Paula?"

"Well, she lives in that old van like an ascetic."

"Because she's dedicated her life to space travel."

"Our space thing is just a game. No, I have a bad feeling about Paula. Something's not right. She's hiding things from me."

"Mysterious women are the best."
"Oh, Dad. Go and clean your room."

20
Emily

A house to herself! Emily lugged a box of groceries into the kitchen. Her mother had been at school from morning till night for three days now, working on her version of a space station. With the help of some art students, she had already designed several rooms, including a dormitory with hammocks, a kitchen of sorts and a bathroom equipped with a camping toilet and an old bathtub. All these items had been donated by parents.

"A bathtub?" Emily had asked. "You know what happens to water in weightlessness, don't you?"

But the most important thing was that her mother was busy. Emily was looking forward to a cosy evening. She would eat salad, play a game of online chess, and maybe Ruben would drop by later. Emily opened her laptop to find a recipe for honey mustard sauce. An email was waiting in her inbox. "Mars 2030" was the subject. Emily opened the message.

Hi Emily,
My name is Eik and I've seen your astronaut training videos. I took part in a TV show that was looking for candidates to colonise Mars. The whole thing was set up like a casting show, I'm sure you've heard of it. Unfortunately it was cancelled because the production company ran out of money, but some of us want to carry on. We have the support of two retired ESA astronauts and we are also working with universities. Our plan is to send a group of people to Mars in 2030. We are currently in talks with a sponsor and if we can convince them, money will no longer be a problem. Everything then depends on finding suitable candidates. We are not looking for daredevils. That's why we want to meet Paula. She is different from those who usually apply to us. We think she would be an enrichment to the team. Could you put us in touch with her? We would love to meet her.
Kind regards,
Eik

Emily looked up from her laptop and cooled her forehead on the mustard jar. Her project was beginning to take shape.

21

Jonathan

At first, Jonathan thought he was seeing a fata morgana, caused by the fogged up lenses of his goggles. He turned onto his back, kept kicking water, took off his goggles, rinsed them and put them back on - all without stopping for a second. But when he looked through the now clear goggles, Ollie was still there. He was lounging in a deck chair with his trouser legs rolled up. A poloshirt with brightly coloured military patches stretched across his stomach.

I'll carry on, Jonathan thought. I won't interrupt my training for him. If Ollie wants to talk, I'll make him talk to me. He can jump into the water and try to keep up with my pace. But what would he want? Prepare the next scam? And he dares to come here? The guy really is audacity personified.

Jonathan swam another thirty laps and got out of the water at the shallow end of the pool. From here it was a short walk to the showers. He had almost reached the door when Ollie started to move. He had obviously realised that Jonathan had no intention of greeting him.

"Hey, wait."

Barefoot, Ollie skidded towards Jonathan, waving his arms to keep his balance. He looked like a penguin dressed up in preppy clothes.

Jonathan let the door to the men's shower fall shut behind him, but Ollie pushed it open again and followed him. A good salesman wasn't so easy to shake off.

"You all right?" Ollie asked.

"You really don't want to know. Did I do something to you at school that I deserve revenge for? I don't think so."

"What do you mean?"

"Don't tell me you came to get the money back."

"Yes, that's why I'm here. But I wanted to return the whole amount, not just my share." In the mist of the showers, Ollie's face was as red as a ripe apple. "Cash out, cash in."

"What do you mean when you say 'my share'?"

"I'm talking about the small interest-free loan. It came at just the right time. I had this great opportunity to take over a colleague's business before it was auctioned off, and I was still five thousand dollars short. But you know how banks are. That's why I decided to help myself in an unbureaucratic way. I knew I'd get it all back, and it worked out even faster than I thought. Two deals in the last few days and here is the cash."

Ollie reached for the back of his trousers.

"Leave it," Jonathan said. "If you don't pay it back in full, there's no point."

"Now you're being greedy. We've known each other a long time, but I never said anything about inviting you. Nor have I ever suggested that you spend the cash. Where would that get us? It's taxpayers' money, after all."

Ollie wagged his finger reprovingly. "Besides, the cost-benefit calculation just doesn't add up. At least not for me. I mean, I have a business in town and a reputation to lose. For a ridiculous sum I will not risk that. Apparently you are. Well, well, gone is gone, as my father used to say. Did you do something nice with it?"

Jonathan wrapped his arms around himself. Suddenly he felt cold, despite the warmth of the room.

"You didn't take the money from the first aid kit?" he asked.

"I don't steal from friends!"

"But Ollie, I didn't take it either!"

"Are you sure?" Ollie looked down at Jonathan questioningly. "Because I haven't told anyone but you where it is."

Jonathan felt his chest tighten.

"I need some air!" He walked back into the hall, sat down on a plastic chair, rested his forearms on his knees and hung his head. This was how he used to recover after a bad race.

The money must have been found by accident. But both the other coaches and the competitors were clearly unmotivated. None of them would have returned to the hall that evening. Theft by cleaning staff? Unlikely. Judging by the state of the hall, it was cleaned at most once a week. The only suspect left was Paula. She had claimed to have been at home most of the time in recent years. So why did she own the van? Someone like her didn't need a car.

"Have you sold a blue van in the last few weeks?" Jonathan asked.

"Yes, we got rid of one of those. It was really just a spare parts depot."

"What did the buyer look like?"

"I don't know, my employee made the deal."

"Damn."

"But he said something. The buyer paid cash. He checked the bills carefully. He thought it was counterfeit, because the woman seemed rather strange to him. But then everything was fine."

"What seemed strange about her?"

"She was wearing a bathing cap. You probably wouldn't have thought that strange."

"Probably not." Jonathan laughed bitterly.

Neither of them said a word for a while.

"Well, my friend," Ollie said at last. "You must pay your debts. I'm afraid I can't help you. But I know a pawnbroker..."

"No need. I've come to a new agreement with Mrs Bunte. The programme will continue and I'll work for free."

"So I can keep my share of the budget?"

"Dream on, you really haven't contributed anything. But you can't just pay the money back. It's officially invested."

"So what do I do with it?"

"Spend it on space travel. Think about it. I just don't have the mind for it at the moment."

Ollie patted Jonathan on the shoulder. "Get some rest, mate. You're training too hard."

Jonathan couldn't sleep that night. Anger and

disappointment kept him awake. Paula had betrayed him. All this time Jonathan had blamed Ollie for taking the money and making him look guilty.

But Paula was the criminal. She hadn't even had the decency to disappear. Instead, she let Jonathan coach her. Was she secretly amused by his naivete? What thrill did it give her? She had even accompanied him to his father's house. And then the fake drowning and the sentimental stories about her anxiety attacks! But Jonathan wasn't going to put up with that. From now on he would use her acting skills for his own benefit. He would make her swim across the lake. Emily would provide video evidence and Jonathan would become Viv's coach again. That would give him at least part of his old life back.

Now he just had to keep his cool and not let his anger and disappointment show.

22

Christiane Mühlheim, Paula's mother

Christiane couldn't make sense of her daughter's latest note. She had read it three times on the computer and then printed it out so that she had a hard copy and could do some underlining. At school, this technique had sometimes helped her to comprehend tasks. With different coloured pens, she sat down at the kitchen table and went through the lines again.

"Astronaut Valentin Vitalievich Lebedev had already spent several months on the space station when he was assigned the onion experiment. Onion bulbs were to be planted to test whether a plant would grow from them. But the astronauts couldn't resist the fresh vegetables and ate the onions - with some bread.

Of course, at some point ground control asked how the experiment was going. The onions were growing very well, the astronauts assured them. When ground control asked a second time, they added: 'The onions are growing fantastically!' Each time, Lebedev and his colleagues became more enthusiastic about the alleged growth of the plants, and eventually ground control became suspicious. Super vegetables in zero gravity? This seemed odd to them, they inquired, and eventually the astronauts were caught out.

That could be my story.

Nothing can be made out of nothing".

Christiane stared at the text, which was now coloured: onions (red), astronauts (blue) and ground control (green). Obviously Paula had identified with one of these groups. But which one?

Christiane was worried. But that didn't help anyone.

"Enough secret reading," she said. "Time for a visit."

That afternoon, Christiane met Paula at a country inn where they were the only guests. They ordered waffles with cream and cherries. While waiting for their food, they watched sheep grazing outside the window.

"How's it going with the people from Airbnb?" Paula asked.

"Ah, well, they take some getting used to."

"Do you miss me?"

"A little."

Christiane smiled wryly. She would have liked to put Paula in the car and take her back. How was her daughter? Paula's cheeks were flushed. She looked like someone who had spent a lot of time outdoors.

"It was good that I finally moved out," Paula said. "You have to stand on your own two feet at some point."

"But this astronaut training seems hard. Aren't you overdoing it?"

"Why?"

"I've seen the videos," Christiane said.

Had she given herself away? She knew about the videos from Paula's notes. But her daughter didn't seem suspicious.

"This is a big deal for Emily," she said. "She's earning money now from advertising. Just like I used to."

"You don't run your blogs anymore?"

"No, I do what you would call serious work now."

"Really?"

Christiane tried to put on a surprised face. There was no mention of her daughter's new job in the videos. So it should better be news to Christiane.

The waffles were served. Christiane scooped up some cream and thought about how to be a kind and supportive mother. You should compliment the children, talk kindly about what they were doing, ask questions until you knew exactly what they were up to, and then you could talk shop together.

"Did you buy the van that you are now living in?" Christiane asked.

"Yes, of course. Do you think I stole it?"

Paula raised her eyebrows.

Confused, Christiane put down her fork. What was wrong with the question?

"I mean, you could rent it or borrow it," she said.

"Dad's mad because I didn't take it for a test drive, isn't he?"

"I think so. You know how he is."

Paula nodded.

"It's good to have you here." Christiane made a sweeping gesture with her arm, as if the flat land around her belonged to a kingdom over which Paula reigned. "And the waffles are delicious."

"Is there something you want to tell me, Mum?"

"I didn't realise how well you swim."

"Are you kidding? My technique is a disaster and I've either freaked out or turned back early in every video so far."

"Does the coach know about your special challenge?"

"About my fear, you mean. Yes, I've talked to him about it."

"But does he realise what it means?"

"How could he? You can't understand it unless you experience it. Besides, understanding doesn't help me. Torben was understanding. And seven months later he got married in Sydney."

Paula had been seeing Torben for two years. After school he had gone on a trip around the world without her.

"I just need a few more weeks of rest," Paula had said. "Then I'll come and see you."

The weeks had turned into months. Torben had met a surf instructor and broken up with Paula.

"That won't happen to me again," Paula said. "This time I'll fight."

For the swimming instructor? Christiane preferred not to ask. She should have made a list of all the information she must not have known. They'd better talk about the astronaut project, that was safe territory.

"You've been so busy lately," Christiane said. "You hardly ever went out before, and now you live all alone in the van and travel long distances."

"This isn't New York," Paula said. "There are twenty people per square metre here."

"Still."

Christiane had finished her waffle. Her coffee cup was already empty. In a moment the waitress would come and ask if they wanted anything else. Paula would probably say no, and then it would be time to go. Christiane finally had to say what was on her mind, even if it didn't sound good.

"You wouldn't really get on a rocket, would you?" she asked.

"You can't ride a bicycle into space."

"But it's dangerous, especially for someone like you. You could die."

"We train to avoid that."

"But you can also have an anxiety attack in the water."

"I can have an attack anywhere, that much I've understood by now. And that's why it's no use hiding."

Paula had spoken loudly. Probably the waitress couldn't help but eavesdrop.

Christiane sat back, closed her eyes and shook her head. Pictures of Paula as a toddler flashed through her mind.

At the age of two, Paula had insisted on having a blanket to sleep under, which she pulled up to her nose. At the age of three, she started building caves.

"Quite normal," the teachers said. "Children love that."

But Paula would not tolerate other children in her den; she built her hiding places so that only she could fit in.

At primary school, she insisted on sitting in the back row in the corner.

"Because you want to keep an eye on things?" the teacher asked.

"No," Paula said. "I don't want to be seen when the ghoul comes."

When the teacher told Christiane about this, she was taken aback. "She never mentioned the ghoul to me before."

"I got the feeling she was embarrassed," the teacher said. "She thinks she knows there's no such thing as a ghoul and that it's all in her head. She confided in me because she thinks I know everything. Including how to chase the ghoul away. Maybe you should see a psychologist."

But Paula didn't want that. There was nothing wrong with her, she had said. Christiane still wondered if Paula had hidden her symptoms to avoid being seen as ill. On the surface, Paula was a happy girl. Although she liked to spend time alone in her room, she had friends, and at school she played the violin in the school choir. She performed solo at parties.

"Don't you get stage fright?" Christiane asked.

"A little. But that's normal, isn't it?"

"No visits from the ghoul?"

"Please don't mention that again!"

Paula needed peace and quiet sometimes, she wanted her private space to retreat to, but as long as she had that, everything was fine.

But then came the school trip. Christiane had to pick Paula up from a camp in the Bavarian Forest after three days. The teacher's description had sounded dramatic: Paula had collapsed and could not get out of bed.

The doctor examined her thoroughly and found nothing physically wrong. But Paula continued to complain of dizziness. Low blood pressure was not uncommon in growing girls, but the dizziness occurred in atypical situations, such as when Paula was sitting on the sofa watching television.

A psychologist eventually asked Paula a series of questions, and when Paula answered "yes" to most of them, her condition was given a name: "Generalised Anxiety Disorder".

"But I'm not afraid in these situations," Paula said.

"You're just experiencing the physical symptoms of anxiety," the psychologist said. "It is the body's way of dealing with stress. Some people get stomachaches or have trouble sleeping, you get heart palpitations and sweat. Do you worry a lot? Do you often think about dying and are you depressed?"

"Yes. But that's normal, isn't it?"

Paula's eyes darkened. Her world view must have changed at that moment. So most of the others weren't secretly fighting with the ghoul? They were really so happy and carefree?

"Your daughter is sensitive to stress," said the psychologist.

But how to avoid heartbreak and maths problems?

"If there's anything I can do to help..." Christiane said as they drove home.

Paula shook her head. She didn't want any help, she just wanted to be normal. It reassured her to know that there was nothing wrong with her body and that her condition could be alleviated with medication if necessary. She wasn't interested in therapy. It wasn't that bad. For the rest of her time at school, anxiety was not a problem. But after the last exam, Paula announced that she didn't want to do anything for a few weeks. Doing nothing meant staying in her room and watching TV. In the autumn of that year, she started the first of her internet projects, which from then on she referred to as her "work".

"But you have to get out," Christiane said. "And be with people."

Paula didn't understand her. She was with people, in virtual company. Christiane had spent endless hours with Bernhard discussing how their daughter could become independent, and they had finally decided to push Paula out of the nest so that she could fly.

Christiane doubted that this was the right decision. The space was too big for her daughter. Paula would soon realise that. And then? If things didn't work out, she wanted to hide. Where could she do that now?

Christiane waved to the waitress and asked for the bill.

"If you ever have any problems with the van," she said to Paula. "Come back home. This Airbnb rental was a stupid idea."

"That's nice of you, but I'm not moving back in with you."

Paula pulled her wallet out of her pocket and insisted on treating Christiane. As she fumbled for coins she said: "I'm in a new orbit now."

23

Emily

Emily climbed onto Paula's van, an open book in her hand.
"Forgot your homework?" Paula asked. "Reading in a car makes me sick."
"Me too, but I still want to do it, I've failed German so many times."
"Why don't you set a homework reminder on your phone? I'm sure there's an app for that."
"I didn't forget, I just didn't have time yesterday because I had to advise Mrs Bunte. Her social media manager has the flu and the Facebook page had to be set up."
"What kind of page?"
"Information about the astronaut programme. She wants to upload photos of the space station my mum built."
"Is it finished?
"Including the airlock and control room."
"Sounds like you could really get that thing into space."
"Oh, the control room is made of e-waste." Emily rolled her eyes. Reluctantly she added: "Although it looks pretty real."
"I'm going to go check it out later. But don't forget the German for now. What are we reading?"
"The Rider on the White Horse." Emily sank back into her seat. "I told you about Eik, didn't I?"
"A character in the book?" Paula asked.
"No! Eik is a Dutchman who was in a casting show for the colonisation of Mars."
"That... Yes, I saw a couple of episodes. But it was cancelled after one season, right?"
"Exactly. But beyond the TV screen the project continues. They've even set the year for the first flight: 2030. They're just looking for candidates. That's why he wrote to me. He wanted to talk to you. But I forwarded his e-mail to Mrs Bunte, because all press work is now to be done by the office. I think

Eik has misunderstood something. You're nowhere near ready to put on a space suit.

"But I'm pretending to be," Paula said. "And Mrs Bunte doesn't have any other astronauts apart from me. So she's going to send Eik to me. OMG."

Paula blinked, braked and steered the bus to the side of the road.

"What's going on?" asked Emily.

" I just need to rest."

"You look pale."

"I'll be right back. Can you open the door, please?"

Emily did Paula the favour. Paula put her hands on her thighs, bowed her head and seemed to be meditating.

After a while she straightened up and said: "All right. Close the door and we can continue."

"Are you sure?"

"Yes, it's over."

"What is it?"

"I was afraid."

"Of Eik?"

"Of 2030."

"You can just say no to the adventure."

"Then it's all over."

"Nonsense. You just won't go to Mars."

"But I'm already there. I can't go back." Paula gave Emily a desperate look. "I realise that now. The flight path was miscalculated and I'm only finding out now. I don't have enough fuel to go back. I'm going to fly until the engines fail and then I'm going to die."

"Are you freaking out right now?"

"Not at all. I can see my future. But it's so miserable that I can only describe it in astronaut terms."

"You might make an emergency landing."

"Excuse me?"

"Space is not empty. If you don't go to Mars, you might find another nice planet."

"But if I land on it, I won't be able to get off."
"Then make yourself comfortable."

24
Paula's online notebook

Make myself comfortable? Where? I'm in the van and I'm thinking: breathe in, breathe out! I've taken my pupils to school and I'm going to take them back. I'm functioning.

I can keep my anxiety at bay by concentrating on what needs to be done next: buying food, sweeping the van, doing the laundry at the launderette. But I can't look into the distance.

Do I want to go into space? I never thought that would ever be on the agenda. But then this Dutchman comes round the corner with a serious offer. What should I do?

I've got myself into something. It's only because I'm in love with Jonathan that I'm playing along with this astronaut nonsense. But neither Jonathan nor I are qualified. I even fail the swim, which is supposed to prepare me for weightlessness. I made it past the rock yesterday, but the extra distance was two metres. At this rate, I won't have swum across the lake until the end of next year. By then even Jonathan will have lost his patience. I don't know why he's training with me at all. At first I hoped he wanted to spend time with me, but then our relationship cooled off. He doesn't even look me in the eye anymore, and he always wears this pinched expression around his mouth. It's like he can't control himself not to shout at me. I know I'm a terrible swimmer. He should just tell me so and give up.

I won't give up. As long as Jonathan wants to keep training me, I'll keep swimming. He pretends to believe in me and I pretend to believe that he believes in me. I cling to the illusion that I can be anything I want to be. But I am a failure.

No, wait, I have a skill that astronauts need: I can deal with loneliness. I can suffer and I don't get cabin fever when I see the same four walls day in, day out.

I'll put that to good use.

25

Jonathan

Jonathan pulled up to Emily's house. Emily was waiting outside.

"Is the van broken?" he asked.

"No."

"Then why did I come here?"

"To pick me up."

"Is Paula waiting at the lake?"

"No, she's at the school. She wants to practice there today."

"I didn't know you had a pool."

"We don't. But we do have a space station, built by my mother and some unfortunate children who didn't know what they were getting into when they chose 'creative design' for project days."

"And what is Paula doing in the space station?"

"Let her explain that herself." Emily tapped her camera bag. "My job is just to take you to her and film the training."

The space station had been built on the edge of the school garden and looked as if it had been constructed from a child's drawing. Some of the walls were crooked and the proportions weren't right. Mariella had obviously got extra windows from somewhere and built them in like a wall. But there was only enough material for the left wing of the station. In the middle was the actual greenhouse, and to the right was a corrugated iron shed. A collapsible plastic play tunnel led to it. Where it joined the shed, someone had painted a tendril of flowers on the metal. There was a chimney on the roof, which had been crocheted around, but only up to a height of ten centimetres. The needleworkers seemed to have left early.

Jonathan crossed his arms. "This is ridiculous. I'm not going in there."

One of the first lessons you learned as a coach was to always keep the high ground. When my charges wanted to get out of it, they came up with the wildest ideas. They'd ask to watch videos of the competition, or discuss how to hold their hand in the crawl while bringing it forward in the air for the next stroke (it didn't matter, the hand just had to get back in the water quickly). They did all this just to buy time and avoid a lane or two.

"Paula!" Emily knocked on the greenhouse. Inside, the room was divided by panels. The frame of a hammock protruded from behind one of them. There was a squeak and then Paula appeared. Her cheek had the imprint of pillow creases. She was wearing a white overall. Her lips were moving.

"What?" Emily called out.

Paula walked to the wall and opened a window.

"I said: I'm not coming out."

"Then I'll go again," Jonathan said. "Next time, let me know earlier if I can cut short the drive to see you."

"Can we talk for a minute?"

"We're already doing that."

"Without the public."

Emily looked up from her camera, on which she was changing the battery. "I'm not filming yet."

"Just five minutes, Emily," Jonathan said. "I'm not going to put up with this nonsense any longer than that."

"Okay..." With her camera, Emily trotted off towards the school building.

"So what's this all about?" Jonathan asked.

"I'm concentrating on my core skills," Paula said.

"Lounging around in a greenhouse?"

"It's an isolation experiment. I want to see how long I can survive on my own in the space station. ESA and the Russians did similar tests near Moscow a few years ago."

"I heard about that. They wanted to simulate a flight to Mars and locked a group of people up for 500 days with food rations. But you're all alone and in a greenhouse."

"The Russian station was also pretty cheap. It looked like a sauna from the inside. And the fact that I'm alone makes it even harder. "

"Do you have any food?"

"I will provide that. I plan to leave the station every day for short exploratory walks." She whispered: "I can't cancel the school bus trips, that's what I do for a living."

"What about our swimming lessons?"

"I've thought of a solution for that."

Paula disappeared and returned a short time later with a skateboard.

"You're not serious," said Jonathan.

But Paula lay on her stomach on the board and made swimming movements.

"It's harder on your back than in the water," she gasped. "Is my technique OK?"

"Pretty bad," Jonathan said.

Paula continued anyway. She rowed with her arms and legs until she was dripping with sweat.

After five minutes she gave up. "I can't go on."

"Now get into the back position," Jonathan said. "Put your hands behind your head and do a crawl leg kick. Keep the tension in your core!"

And Paula really tried to follow his instructions. Jonathan watched her through the glass of the greenhouse, growing angrier by the minute.

26
Paula's online notebook

I don't think Jonathan is enthusiastic about the new training methods. Although I have found some exercises on the internet. Core stabilisation is so important! But Jonathan seems to be old school, he's a grinder and believes that a lot helps a lot. Long distances can't be covered in the station. At the end of the session we practised the butterfly. I sat on the skateboard and pushed myself backwards with my heels. After two lanes, which is five metres here, I collapsed.

Sometimes I join in the fun," said Jonathan. "But enough is enough. We'll meet again tomorrow at the lake."

"I'm serious about this experiment," I said.

"You're a clown in an aquarium."

"I'm doing science."

"You haven't even set a goal. How long are you going to stay in there? Until a branch breaks through the roof in the first autumn storm? Until you freeze to death in the winter?"

"Until I've earned a thousand euros from the entrance fees?" The idea came to me spontaneously. "People can visit me for two euros. I'll donate the money to the Chaos Computer Club satellite." I raised my fist. "Freedom! Independent communication!"

In my head I calculated how many students attended Emily's school. Two hundred? Even if they all visited me - which I didn't think they would, because they could see through the glass walls for free - I wouldn't reach the required number. I wouldn't be able to do it next month, or next term, or even this decade.

I need time and patience to do what I want to do. Is my goal to stay in the ward forever? No, just until Jonathan comes. He doesn't seem to have any romantic feelings for me at the moment, but that will change. There are lots of fascinating women out there, but there's only one astronaut within a few hundred kilometres - me. I'm the only one, so he has to fall in love with me. It happens all the time on real space stations. If you spend a lot of time together and have a common goal, it's inevitable that you'll fall in love. If you spend a lot of time together and have a common goal, it's inevitable that you'll become attracted to each other. It's just a law of physics. I will be the sun and Jonathan will be circling around me.

27

Jonathan

Paula had been living on the space station for two weeks and Jonathan was at his wits' end. Viv's performance was getting worse and worse and her parents had now realised what a poor choice the American had been. They looked around for other coaches. Jonathan soon had to win his bet on the lake.

He went to the space station every other day and had Paula do exercises on the roller board. She also jumped rope to build up her stamina. There was no doubt that Paula was getting fitter, but if she couldn't get out in the water and show what she could do, it was all for nothing. Jonathan thought she was playing a game. Emily claimed that Paula only left the station for the school bus rides, but he couldn't verify that.

"Isn't it illegal to live permanently on school grounds?" Jonathan had said to Emily.

"Maybe," Emily sighed, "but my mother is dating the caretaker."

Emily wasn't happy about Paula's isolation experiment either.

"I'm running out of subjects for videos. All I can do is film Paula doing push-ups or lying in a hammock. My fans want more action again.

At the mention of the fans, Jonathan had an idea. Paula wanted to leave the station as soon as she had collected 1000 euros in entrance fees. This could happen sooner than she thought. Jonathan and Emily would organise an open house, where hopefully the fans would turn up in force. Mrs Bunte would also get the publicity going. Such an event would be a good conclusion to the project. They could also invite Eik.

"Are we going to tell Paula?" Emily asked.

"That would only disturb her isolation," Jonathan replied grimly. "Let's surprise her."

The open day was to be held this Saturday. Jonathan thought about contributing money himself if they couldn't raise 1000 Euros. He could borrow some from his dad. Although he hated asking him, he would get over it to get away from Paula. After she left the station, he would give her two weeks. If she hadn't managed to swim across the lake by then, he'd give up on her. It would all be for nothing, and Jonathan would probably never coach Viv again in her entire career, but he would finally be free to try and forget about Paula. Jonathan tried hard to be professional and cool with her, but she must have guessed his true feelings. He was angry with himself. It was stupid to fall in love with a woman who stole, lied and made you turn up several times a week to watch her swimming drills.

But it had all started well! Jonathan remembered Paula wearing her swimming cap as if it were a normal headgear for professional development. He thought back to the underwater exercises in the pool, to Paula's determination that had almost been her fatal flaw, and to the wake-up calls that had often awakened him in anticipation at 5 a.m. Jonathan had thought he had found his soul mate. But this woman was just crazy, unpredictable and seemed to enjoy taking advantage of him.

But he was not going to let her. She would cross the lake for him, or fail in her attempt. Either way, Jonathan would be gone and would never see Paula again.

28
Emily

Mariella had set up tents in the garden for the open day. In case Paula wanted to know what they were for, Emily had prepared a story about an artists' meeting. But Paula didn't ask. She was quiet and seemed depressed when she picked Emily up from school and took her home. Emily hoped that Eik's visit would cheer Paula up a bit. They had originally wanted to hold the open day on the school grounds, but the janitor had vetoed the plan.

"This is really going too far. There are no toilets outside, we don't have a security policy for external events and I don't get paid for weekend work."

So the visitors would drop in at Mariella and Emily's and then take a tour of the space station at the school.

On Saturday morning, Mrs Bunte and another member of staff unloaded boxes of leaflets from their cars.

The first of Emily's fans arrived just after nine. They had brought picnic rugs and barbecues, and Emily had to sign autographs on their mobile phone cases. Eik arrived at ten. He was wearing a silver jacket with the Mars 2030 logo and wanted to go straight to Paula. Emily thought about it. Jonathan hadn't arrived yet and she had wanted to go to Paula's with him. But maybe it would be better if everyone didn't visit the space station at the same time. After all, Paula was still completely clueless.

"I'd better go first," Emily said to Eik as they stood in front of the space station.

He nodded. Emily knocked on the window. "Hello Paula, can I come in?"

"It's open," came the reply.

"She must be in a good mood," Emily said. "You just have to go through this tunnel."

She had been worried that Eik would laugh when she crawled through the play tube, but he just looked at the construction with interest and took a photo.

Emily found Paula in one of the hammocks.

"Did I miss something?" Paula asked. "It's the weekend, isn't it?"

"Yes, Saturday, nothing's wrong. There's no training until tomorrow. I've come for a surprise."

"And?" Paula lifted her head suspiciously. "Don't tell me the Dutchman is here."

"Yes, he's outside. And that's not all."

Emily told them about the open day.

But Paula hardly seemed to take in the news.

"Eik wants to come in?"

"Just to say hello. He's nice."

"So he's serious." Paula stared at Emily with wide eyes. "This Project 2030 - it's no joke."

"No, but neither is our project. You live in primitive conditions, you swim in a cold lake. It's all for progress."

"But I'm not a real astronaut."

"Not yet. But I believe in you, and I'm not the only one."

Emily tried to smile encouragingly.

"I want to hide," Paula said.

"Eik has come all the way from abroad. Talk to him for at least five minutes. I'll bring him in now, OK?"

Paula didn't answer. Instead, her eyes searched the walls as if she wanted to disappear through a second exit. Emily hurried to wave Eik inside. Was she doing the right thing? Her videos had helped to spread the image of Paula as an astronaut. Maybe she had created a version of Paula that had only existed as an idea before. But didn't they say: Fake it until you make it?

Eik came in and rubbed his knees. Emily introduced him to Paula.

"I'm so pleased!" he said. "I've brought presents."

He opened a backpack and took out a DVD. "Video greetings from the team. A T-shirt. And here - if you want to join in - our communicator."

He handed Paula a sturdy looking headset. With the DVD and T-shirt already in her hands, she had no choice but to put it on.

"You can use it to contact us wherever you are. There's a number pad on the right ear and a speed dial for each team member." He winked. "Even if you don't take off any time soon, your connection to the ground station is already guaranteed."

Paula seemed almost desperate now. She looked past Eik out of the window.

We should have come here with Jonathan first, Emily thought.

29
Paula's online notebook

They're off again. They wanted to give me an hour's rest before the sightseeing tour with Emily's fans. How kind. I'm still wearing the headset and feel like I've been crowned Miss Space with it, even though I didn't stand out from the crowd of my fellow contestants in either the evening gown round or the swimsuit part. Haha, especially the swimsuit part. What does Eik want from me? I asked him. He says that he admires my attitude. I don't let difficulties stop me.

But does that mean I want to die as a pioneer, on a flight to Mars with no way back and no certainty of ever getting there?

I think of poor Komarov. The Russians were going to shoot him into orbit on Soyuz 1 in 1967. His replacement was to be none other than Yuri Gagarin. But a few days before the launch, Gagarin inspected the spacecraft and discovered more than 200 technical problems. He asked Soviet leader Leonid Brezhnev to postpone the flight, but Brezhnev was determined to give his people something to celebrate the sixth anniversary of Gagarin's first trip into space.

The launch had to go ahead as planned. Komarov probably suspected that he would not return alive, but he did not want to refuse to protect his friend Gagarin, who would otherwise have had to take his place. It was terrible. Shortly after reaching orbit the first technical problems occurred. On their fifth orbit, ground control ordered Komarov to land as soon as possible. But then they lost contact with him. The Soyuz orbited the Earth seven more times before the staff were able to reach their cosmonaut again. On the 16th orbit, Gagarin ordered Komarov to return because the fuel was running low. The Soyuz should have landed under automatic control, but this failed. Komarov had to steer manually. That also went wrong. The main parachute, which should have glided the capsule back to Earth, did not open at all, and the reserve parachute only partially deployed.

Komarov and his capsule were smashed to pieces at a speed of 144 km/h.

Allegedly, American intelligence overheard all of Komarov's messages to ground control station. Komarov is said to have realised early on that he was going to die. He said goodbye to his wife in tears. In his last seconds, he hurled wild insults at the mission commanders.

I wish I had never heard this story. People like to remember successful missions. But many successes are preceded by losses.

Are all astronauts suicidal? If you decide to go around Mars without a return ticket, you shouldn't have anything to keep you on Earth. Eik probably realised that this was the case with me. Jonathan didn't show up. Why didn't he come to the open day? Apparently he doesn't care about me anymore. He's probably only made the wake-up calls out of a sense of duty, knowing that I'll be leaving this planet in the not too distant future.

The headset feels like it's part of my skull. Infinite void, here I come.

30

Christiane Mühlheim, Paula's mother

"I'm going to Paula's," Christiane called to her husband from the kitchen. "Don't wait for me for dinner."

"But we wanted to spend this afternoon together -"

"Sorry, I'm in a hurry. I've waited far too long."

After reading Paula's last note, Christiane was deeply worried. This Komarov story was a cry for help! Christiane had to do something. Why didn't Paula know about the open day? Emily had announced it on her channel. But Paula probably didn't watch the videos of herself. Why should she? She had been there live.

In the stairwell, Christiane took two steps at once. Luckily, she had parked in front of the door. She typed Emily's address into the navigation system and started her car. The calculated travel time was 34 minutes. She would speed up!

When Christiane arrived at Emily's house, there was a barbecue in the garden and a group of schoolchildren were painting a two-metre silhouette of a rocket. A woman in a colourful man's shirt was dragging a sculpture around. The scene looked like a cross between a children's birthday party and an open-air exhibition.

"I'm looking for Emily," Christiane said to a girl.

She was led to the back of the house, where Emily was standing with two men, showing them something on a tablet. One of the men was wearing a silver jacket. The other was Jonathan.

"I'm Paula's mother."

She wanted to greet him, but in her excitement the movement she made was more like a flick of the wrist. Jonathan backed away. Only when he had obviously understood that Christiane had no intention of hitting him, did he shake her hand.

"Nice to meet you..."

"We don't have time for formalities," Christiane said. "You urgently need to read something. May I?"

She took the tablet from Emily and logged into Paula's notebook.

"Come with me," she said to Jonathan.

She raised her finger and pointed at Emily and the man in the silver jacket. "Just him."

No one dared speak out against her parental firmness.

Jonathan followed her to a bench by a garden pond and the other two trudged off to join the other guests.

Christiane had opened the first note, but then she remembered that there wasn't enough time for Jonathan to read everything. She scrolled down to the last few lines about Komarov.

"This one!"

Jonathan read, muttering.

"That's terrible," he said. "I didn't know about that."

"Yes, it's terrible," Christiane said. "But read the last sentence: Infinite void, here I come."

"It's just a phrase," said Jonathan.

"My daughter loves you. But because you don't seem to return her feelings, she wants to sign up for a suicide mission."

"Space travel is very safe now. Paula's chances of reaching Mars alive are good."

"But she can never come back from there. Stop her!" Christiane grabbed Jonathan's shoulders.

"Calm down," he said. "You're acting as if Paula is going to leave tomorrow. But 2030 is still over ten years away. She could change her mind many times in that time."

"But she won't. I know my daughter."

"What do you think I should do?"

"Talk to her."

"We have a wake-up call every morning and we train several times a week. But that's about it. I think it's asking a lot of me to work with her at all. I have lost my swimming groups because of her. Did you know that Paula stole the money for the van?

Christiane let go of Jonathan. "She used it to buy a vehicle to live in during her astronaut training. So the money wasn't misappropriated."

"Then the van doesn't belong to her."

"Did she say that? She just lives in it. Besides, it certainly wasn't her intention to put you out of work."

Jonathan seemed to be thinking about this argument. Christiane was about to ask him again to talk to Paula when Emily came running in.

"She's gone!"

"Paula?" asked Jonathan.

"Yes. I couldn't reach her on the phone.

My mother called the janitor and he checked the ward. She's not there. Her van is gone too."

"We can show the visitors around without her," Jonathan said.

"Forget the tour. I'm worried about Paula doing something stupid. You should have seen her when she met Eik. She wasn't prepared for him at all. We should have warned her."

"What's going to happen?" asked Jonathan. "It's not like Eik brought any rockets with him that Paula could use to catapult herself into orbit. She probably just wants some peace and quiet and to get away from it all. Go underground for a moment".

He faltered at the last words.

"Oh no," Emily said.

She and Jonathan looked at each other.

"She won't be at the lake, will she?" Christiane asked.

But she thought she knew the answer.

31

Paula

Paula stood on the shore of the lake. She had never been here alone before. But why not? She could have trained herself by staying close to the shore. But it wasn't the same.

You couldn't simulate everything. You couldn't launch a rocket at half speed as a test. You had to be brave and take your chances.

She should have just told Jonathan she loved him. He would probably have been embarrassed and mumbled something about "keeping work and home separate". But that would have been just an excuse to make Paula feel less bad. They had never really got to know each other. There were too many miles between ground control station and the astronaut. But Paula could show Jonathan what she was made of. She would swim across the lake or sink trying. She wanted Jonathan to see what she was capable of. And she wanted to see for herself.

In the van, Paula changed into her wetsuit. She had to remove her headset. Thoughtfully, she turned it over in her hand. Should she put it back on? She could call Eik and ask him to put her through to Emily. The girl had accompanied her to every training session and had become a friend. It would be unfair to attempt the swim without her.

Paula's finger circled the number keys. What speed dial did Eik have? She couldn't remember him telling her. But since he seemed to be an important person on 'Mars 2030', he was probably assigned the 1. Paula pressed the number. Nothing happened. The 11? Now there was a brief sound from the headphones and then a crackling noise.

"Hello," someone said.
"Eik?"
"Is that you, Paula?"
"Yes."
"We're looking for you."

"I'm on a mission."

"What?"

"In zero gravity."

Paula heard a chatter of voices in the background.

"Give me that!" There was a rustling. "This is Jonathan."

"Hello ground control.

How's the weather where you are?"

"Funny. Why aren't you in your greenhouse barrack?"

"Astronauts don't go into space to sit around and be stupid. I feel fit." This was a lie. "I'm doing it now."

"You want to swim?"

"Exactly."

"To the rock?"

"All the way."

"No!"

"That was our goal. Why should people pay to see me in a hammock?"

"Okay, Paula..." Jonathan faltered. He wouldn't be able to stop her, and she seemed to realise that. "But at least wait till we get there."

"I'm getting cold."

"Please!"

"Hurry up."

"Hang on."

Paula heard muffled speech. Jonathan was obviously keeping the microphone covered. He didn't have to bother. Paula removed the headset from her ears and hung it around her neck. She needed some peace and quiet to collect herself.

A light wind had come up, rippling the water of the lake. The trees across the water seemed impossibly far away. Paula thought about how tired she had always been when she had reached the rock. And that was only a third of the way. How was she going to manage to swim further into the unknown after that rescue platform?

"I need a fresh start," Paula said to herself. "I'll start on the other side."

That way she would swim to her van, where warm blankets and chocolate were waiting. There was another advantage to this plan: Paula could wait until the others had arrived and Emily had started the camera, but she couldn't be stopped. The water would be between her and Jonathan. Paula took off her flip-flops and laced up her trainers - a good precaution, as it turned out, because the path around the lake was overgrown with nettles in many places.

Paula had to climb over a fallen tree and jump over a stream that flowed into the lake. At least that warmed her muscles. She spotted a bench. Empty bottles and a plastic bag, its colours faded by the sun, were lying around. Soon after, she passed the remains of a wooden footbridge. The planks were weathered. It had been a long time since anyone had left here by boat. Paula stopped. The lake seemed to fall steeper here. That was good. She wanted to wade through as little mud and water plants as possible. About a hundred metres further on she spotted the weeping willow she had only seen from a distance. Paula had reached her starting point. She put the headset back on.

"Where are you?"

"We'll be right there," Jonathan said.

"I'm waiting."

Paula shivered and started to jump. A few minutes later she saw a procession of people arriving on the other side of the river. At the front was someone in a black hoodie.

Paula recognised Jonathan.

"I've spotted you," she said.

"But we don't see you."

"I'm over here." Paula waved.

A rustle, then Emily spoke. "I've zoomed in on you. So, Paula, today's the big day. Anything you want to say to the fans?"

What, Paula thought. Last words?

She thought of Komarov.

"You have to be able to rely on your team," she said.

"Everyone only looks at the astronauts, but those who stay behind on Earth have the harder job. They can only observe and support, but if something goes wrong, they will blame themselves for the rest of their lives."

"That sounds wise, Paula. I'd like to cheer you on, but ground control is signalling me that they want to take over again."

Paula saw Jonathan step up beside Emily. Moments later she heard his voice.

"I'm coming over to you."

"Why?"

"In case you don't make it."

"You don't think I'll even make it halfway?"

"We'd better get some more training in." Jonathan was now on the footpath that went around the lake.

"Stay with the others," Paula called. "I'll jump in now."

"Don't. I've read your diary."

"What?"

"Your notes. Your mother showed them to me."

Paula suddenly felt naked. How much had Jonathan read? Probably the important parts. Then he knew what she had been hiding from him all this time. But what could she say? What could she apologise for? Paula just wanted to get away. Exposed in front of Jonathan, the lake lost its terror.

Paula took off her shoes and waded into the water. Her heart pounded in her throat. She pushed off the bottom with her feet and swam, forcing herself to make calm movements and exhale with each stroke. Her head was now just above the surface and from this perspective the other shore seemed even further away. She would have preferred not to look ahead, but she needed a fixed point to orient herself. She turned her eyes towards the van and tried to squint a little so that her surroundings became blurred. But as soon as she stopped concentrating on her vision, her other senses became sharper. She felt a cross current on her right foot. Had something slipped beneath her? Involuntarily, she moved faster, but now, strangely, she seemed to be moving even slower.

Stay calm, she told herself. Otherwise you'll make mistakes.

She went through the whole breaststroke sequence in her head: Pulling her legs in, straddling, stretching, bringing her arms forward and pushing them towards her body - not to the side, as she had learned as a child, but diagonally downwards, as Jonathan had demonstrated. But her arms didn't seem to be exerting any force on the water. Paula clenched her left fist to reassure herself that her body was still obeying her. When she released her hand, she realised her mistake. Instead of closing her fingers, she had spread them.

As soon as she formed her hands into flat shovels, things went better. Only her breathing was still too fast. If you breathe wrong, you could get a cramp. This prospect didn't help to reassure her. Paula started counting in her head: inhale, 1, 2, 3, hold your breath, 4, 5, exhale, 7, 8, 9. As soon as the pressure in her chest eased, she turned and compared the distance between the two banks. A quarter was done.

32

Jonathan

Jonathan had seen Paula leave something on the shore. He couldn't tell what it was, but he assumed it was her shoes and headset. The moment she ran into the water, his mobile phone rang in his pocket. Jonathan took the headset off Eik's head and answered it. Liv was on the line.

"I'm watching over the internet. She's really doing it! How did you manage that so fast?"

"I don't know," Jonathan admitted.

"I've got to go to the gym for training in a minute. I hope this is my last one with this coach. Next week you're supposed to be on the side of the pool. Root for Paula for me. If I had known she was swimming today, I would have sent her a message. Wishing her good luck and all that.

"That wouldn't have been a good idea. She doesn't know about my bet with your mother."

"What do you mean - she's just splashing around in the cold, dirty pond? Because she likes it?"

"We're simulating a field mission in space," Jonathan said. "I thought you subscribed to Emily's videos. Then you know what they're about."

"But I never have time to watch them." Viv laughed. "Field mission. You guys are really weird. But Paula still needs to work on her technique. Her arm movements are a disaster."

"What is she doing?"

"You can see for yourself. Hey, I have to go in now. Good luck."

She hung up.

Paula had only covered about a third of the distance and seemed to be resting. Jonathan cursed his mild nearsightedness. His eyesight was good enough for the length of a swimming pool lane, but here at the lake, more metres separated him from Paula. He could no longer make out details at this distance. He needed to get back to Emily. Her camera seemed to have a good zoom. He put the headset back on to keep his hands free as he fought his way through the overgrown bushes. There was a splash. Then a gasp. The hairs on his arms stood up as he realised where the sound must have come from. Paula hadn't left the headset on the shore. She was still wearing it, which meant she must have heard the conversation. From what Jonathan had said to Viv, Paula could easily work out what her part in the bet had been.

"Paula," Jonathan said. "Can you hear me?"

No reply.

"Paula!" he shouted across the water. "I'm sorry!"

She made no sign of understanding him.

Jonathan dug his fingernails into his temples. He was such an idiot! He had been angry with Paula all along, condemning her for cheating and completely forgetting how wrong he had been. Paula may not be an astronaut yet, but at least she showed courage. He, on the other hand, failed in everything expected of a ground control employee: Instead of providing information and assistance, he obscured the purpose of the mission. In reality, the 'field mission' served only Jonathan's own interests.

33

Paula

She shouldn't have rushed off. Why on earth did she take the headset? It was clearly not designed for use in the water. Although Paula swam without putting her face in the water, the earpieces had got wet in the first few strokes and didn't make a sound afterwards. She then flipped the microphone up, but it didn't stay in place and sank back down after a few seconds. Paula tried to push the metal ring to the back of her head so that the wet earpieces were on her forehead. This took a little longer but didn't work in the end. Paula used both hands to adjust the position of the headset, dipped up to her nose and swallowed water. When she breathed air again, she thought she heard her name. But it was probably just an illusion. Jonathan was no longer on the path. Nor did she see anyone in a black sweater among those standing on the shore.

He was gone. He had read her notes and decided he wanted nothing more to do with her. Paula's limbs grew heavy. Why was she torturing herself? What was the point? She closed her eyes for three faint breaths. When she opened them again, she didn't seem to be any closer to the shore.

There was a flaw in her mission plan. Real astronauts were always connected to the station with a safety line.

It could be used to pull them back if they let go and threatened to drift away. Space was so big and the space station so small. But maybe some astronauts let go on purpose. Maybe they suddenly saw no point in clinging to the tin can of the station in the face of the infinite void. But Paula let herself drift. Were there currents in a lake? Did you wash up on the shore by yourself at some point, or was that only the case in the sea?

She opened her lips and let the water flow into her mouth. It was drinkable, it tasted of nothing. Here she had everything she needed. And peace and quiet. Especially peace and quiet.

Now there was a commotion on the shore. Why were they

all shouting? Jonathan was back now, taking off his sweater. Not again. Paula didn't want to be rescued. Jonathan would despise her all the more. Paula waved to her audience and gave them a thumbs up. Two people held Jonathan back. They had understood that Paula was all right.

Jonathan broke free and ran towards the van. Was he going to take it? If he did, Paula would have nothing. At least they would be even. Jonathan got in, but then nothing happened. After a while he got out and walked back to the shore.

He wiped his face, as if to wipe the sweat from his brow. Then Paula saw the blood. It was running down Jonathan's eyes and cheeks until he looked like a clown crying red tears.

"What are you doing?" Paula screamed. "Stop it!"

Why didn't anyone intervene? Jonathan was mutilating himself and everyone was watching. Emily had also turned to Jonathan and was filming. It was sick. Paula slipped off the headset and started to crawl.

34
Paula's online notebook

I couldn't go on, but then I did. It wasn't until the last hundred metres, when I realised that everyone's attention was on me and no one was paying attention to Jonathan, so his life wasn't in danger, that my fear for him disappeared and I realised how exhausted I was. The most critical moment of a mission is the return. When a space shuttle re-enters the Earth's atmosphere, it runs the risk of burning up. Its heat shields have to withstand temperatures of more than a thousand degrees.

I had no heat shield, just my wetsuit. As soon as my feet hit the ground, I ran. I almost fell in the last few metres to the shore. My body was no longer used to the force of gravity.

Jonathan came towards me. His eyes were red, as if he had been crying for hours. Blood was trickling down his face and neck.

"What happened?" I asked.

"I shaved my eyebrows," he said.

"What for?"

"When you're standing next to me, you can take off your bathing cap and not be afraid of stupid looks. Everyone will be staring at me. Yuck."

He spat out soap.

"That stuff is everywhere."

"Are you crazy?"

"I've been holding out on you."

"So have I."

We looked at each other.

"Will it jeopardise the mission?" I asked.

"The mission has been successfully completed," he said.

And so it was. I now knew that I could swim across a lake.

I could probably fly to Mars, but I didn't want to. You don't have to do everything that's possible.

But things were possible that I hadn't dared to dream

about. Yes, of course I had dreamed of them. When I kissed Jonathan, he still tasted of honey and lemon.

The open day went on late into the night. I heard that Mariella had applied to join Mars 2030. Emily told me about it the next day. Mr Keunecke was also there. At first Mrs Bunte didn't want to talk to him, but later she was seen opening a bottle of champagne with him. Then she called me and said I could keep the van, it was officially OK, and Mr Keunecke would even have the reverse repaired.

That's good, I need a car. Jonathan will be moving to Munich to train Viv, a talented swimmer. We'll postpone our wake-up calls until late in the morning, when his early training with Viv is over and I've finished my school run. We plan to visit each other every weekend.

We have to drive a few hundred kilometres, but that's no distance - galactically speaking.

MORE BY KIRSTEN BAILEY

Four on the Flour: A Captivating Story about Music, Friendship and Girl Power

My father stood up. He smoothed out the creases in his pants. At that moment I hated him. He was as much mobster as his parents! I felt like an alien adopted by an evil human family.

Imelda loves to sing - just for herself. Her dad is a famous music producer but the glamorous world of the stars scares her off.

One day she accompanies her father, meets three talented sisters and becomes friends with them. Soon, she faces a dilemma. Her father only wants to sign one of the sisters and asks Imelda to mediate. In order not to disappoint her new friends, she makes up a lie.

The four of them start rehearsing for a big festival. Will they finally enter the stage?

Excerpt:

My father stood in front of me. His new briefcase smelled of leather.

"You're coming with me today, Imelda," he said.

"What?" I looked up from my Gameboy, where the Tetris pieces continued to fall mercilessly. "Why?"

My father had never taken me with him when he was away on business. Once I'd overheard him telling a friend on the phone that he'd chosen the music industry to get out and meet people who weren't family.

"Interesting people," he probably meant, or: "People my parents don't know."

We are rich. My father was born rich because my grandparents were in the coffee trade when it was still profitable. Sounds easy going? Well, living in our suburban mansion wasn't as easy going as you might think. Like two

Mafia bosses, Grandma and Grandpa controlled the entire neighborhood. In their homespun web of acquaintances and obligations, they monitored every move, commented on every decision, and if they didn't like something, it had better be changed, pronto.

But in the music business, which had spilled over from Hamburg, that they had no foothold. So my father must have chosen this as the ideal niche for himself. He probably wanted to prove himself, do something of his own and make up for the wild parties that had been forbidden to him in his youth. I had a lot of sympathy for him, but I would have been happier if he had been a tennis manager or a boxing promoter. Music was my thing.

Since I was six years old, I took singing lessons at the music school. I never spoke to my parents about it. They had set up a standing order for the fees, and I sneaked to and from my lesson with Ms Schneider every Thursday without saying a word. Ms Schneider was taciturn and had private problems that made her dependent on my bribes. By the third year, I had convinced her to spare me the annual audition with an extra "Christmas salary". Since then, every December, a portion of my fortunately generous pocket money has been used to keep me out of the audition. Ms Schneider always accepted the envelope with the same words: "Thank you, Imelda, but it's too bad nobody can hear you."

I had a different point of view. My voice was good, and that was exactly why it should be mine and mine alone.

The Gameboy made a sad sound. I had lost.

"If you really want to study," Grandpa had once said. "I'm going to buy a private university, and that's where you'll go."

"Get dressed," my father urged. "I want to be on time for them."

"For whom?" I asked.

"I'll tell you in the car. Come on ..."

He tried to grab my jacket to help us get started, but his hand got caught. For the spring that was about to begin, there were about a dozen jackets. My mother would buy me all the styles if I couldn't decide, often in several colors. She thought it was worth the time saved. And the owner of my favorite boutique was Grandma's best friend, so the money stayed in the family. Occasionally, when overwhelmed, I would stuff my closet into bags, take everything downstairs, and start wearing the same outfit for a week. I regularly felt like a fraud. Everyone knew, and I knew it better than anyone, that I was just pretending that I had nothing to wear.

"It's warm enough," I decided, slipping into my green Chucks. "I don't need a jacket. Let's go."

My dad took the Mercedes because it was in the garage out front. As we rolled down the driveway, past the statues of Greek gods and our Polish gardener who was trimming the boxwoods to form curved columns, my dad wanted to put on a Jacksons Five tape. I let him, but turned the volume down to elevator level.

"So what's the plan?" I asked.

"Simple."

Without making sure the road was clear, my father turned onto it. Such maneuvers had gotten him into a few fender-benders. But apparently saving time was more important here, too. "I have three sisters on my hands. Triplets. Not identical, but with their hairstyles and the way they wear their clothes, they are close enough."

"How great!" I was electrified. "Like the Olson twins with a third sibling?"

My father gave me a satisfied smile. "I knew you'd like it."

It had always been my greatest wish to have a brother or sister, but this was one of the few things that couldn't be bought. Excitedly, I pulled at the loose threads of my pants. I had cut my jeans open at the knees to look like the cool girls on MTV. "And they sing, the three of them?"

"No, they dance." Ignoring a garbage truck that had the right of way, my father yelled over the horn: "That means they are supposed to be dancing. They're still in rhythmic gymnastics, but Fabrice thinks they're moving well and they'll pick up the choreographies quickly."

Fabrice was a dance coach from Paris that my father had recently hired. Together they were working on the comeback of a trio that used to perform in the big discos in the area. But they were hardly booked anymore. So now my father had given up on them too. How sad.

"What's going to happen to Three ..."

"Three for Me will become Four on the Floor." My dad gave me a sideways glance. "What do you think of the name?"

"But with the triplets, there'll be six in the group."

"Nope."

A shark-like grin crossed his face. I let go of my hand on the door and put it back in my lap.

"Okay."

If he thought I was going to ask, he was wrong. At first my father didn't show his impatience, but three blocks away he lost the game and blurted out his idea: "Because only one of the three ever performs."

"Sure," I said. "Why not? Pay the three of them and let one of them work, that sounds pretty smart."

"They are seventeen years old like you, and therefore still minors," my father said. "They're not allowed to work too much or for too long a time. But if they alternate, it doesn't matter. And if one of them gets sick, I've got two more up my sleeve. Or in case of injury. These athletes always have something going on."

He pulled into a neighborhood of townhouses. All the houses looked alike: two and a half stories, red brick, white window frames and doors, as if to foreshadow the triplets. Outside were small gardens with neat flowerbeds, paved sidewalks and neatly trimmed street trees. The setting was reminiscent of a Swedish Lego city. It conveyed warmth and order.

"As for payment..." My father parked between a van and a Beetle. "They only get paid when they're onstage."

"Wow," I said. "What a lousy condition. And the three of them are going to agree to this?"

"Well, convincing them is going to be challenging." My father turned off the engine and put on the parking brake. "For you."

"Nah, forget it." As he got out of the car, I remained seated. "I'm not negotiating for you!"

"I'll do the talking." My father leaned in and whispered: "You're there for the atmosphere. They're more likely to trust someone their own age, and as a family man, I come across as likable."

"Unless they're completely stupid, they'll never sign with you." I shook my head. "Never ever."

"You're so dramatic, Imelda. But that's okay. Be yourself, speak their language, do your teenage thing."

My father stood up. He smoothed out the creases in his pants. I hated him at that moment. He was as much mobster as his parents! I felt like an alien adopted by an evil human family.

"Are you coming?" he asked. "Look, there they are."

From my position in the car, I saw the door of a house open. Socked feet appeared, pant legs that were cut off at the knees like mine, and behind them another pair of pant legs, these ones with frayed hems.

"Hello!" said my father. "I'm back, and this time I brought my daughter."

The heels of his leather shoes clicked on the stone steps. As far as I was concerned, he should lie to the family. I would just sit there until he came out. If it took too long, I'd run in any direction, and if it was the wrong one, I'd get a cab to take me to Granny's so she could pay. Which brings us back to money. Why did my father want to have more of it? Our villa could have had six of these little houses. It wasn't fair. The rich were getting richer. No, I had to see that justice was done and foil my father's evil plan.

I pushed open the car door and got out. In the front yard

there were self-painted eggs hanging in the bushes, and in the window next to the door were three cut-out paper bunnies. Those were elementary school crafts, and since they were probably made by the sisters, they must have been a few years old. I imagined their mother going downstairs in February to the shelf where seasonal decorations were neatly stored. She took out a box marked "Easter," carried it up the stairs, and opened it on the carpet in the living room. At the top was an envelope, from which she took the bunnies, held them up to the light, and smiled softly at the girls' awkward, angular cuts. Touched, she said: "I can still remember exactly who made which one."

Where were my artworks? In other families, they were hanging on the refrigerator, at least temporarily, but the first time I noticed this was at a children's birthday party. I was ten years old and would have found it embarrassing to ask my mother to stick self-painted pictures on the highly polished surfaces of our kitchens. Especially since we ate in the dining room. Only the cook would have seen my work.

Lost in my own thoughts, I tripped over the welcome mat.

"Oops." My father grabbed my arm. "May I introduce you to my daughter, Imelda. And this is Heike, Hanna and Hilke."

He made a gesture that included all the girls. He probably couldn't put the names to the faces. The three of them were a head shorter than me and had long, straight hair. Two of them were brunettes and the third was a blonde.

"Hi," the blonde said. "Cool that you came. We have been so looking forward to seeing you. Your father told us you were a singer."

"Oh... uh..." I was stunned into silence. I didn't like my father mentioning my singing to strangers, especially since he had probably used my hobby as a confidence-building story.

"Our mother is still at work," the blonde said to my father. "Can I offer you a cup of coffee or something?"

"No problemo," my father waved her off. "And thank you very much, a glass of water will be fine. I told Imelda about your trophy collection. She would love to see it."

Excuse me? I turned to him, but his expression was cold. Ah, so now we should go and do our teenage thing and make friends with each other.

"The trophies are upstairs," the blonde said. Under the open collar of her white polo shirt I discovered a gold chain with an inscription. Hanna, aha! The others were wearing name jewelry as well.

Hilke, the one with the longest hair and freckles, beckoned me to follow. To the right of the narrow hallway, a dark red carpeted staircase led to the second floor. On the wall was a photo gallery of the three of them. The oldest photos showed them in the sandbox or in various disguises. From the age of about six, they performed gymnastics in shiny leotards on parallel bars, rings, and over mats. In one of the pictures, they were standing arm in arm with a redhead who looked familiar to me. I wondered who she was. I stopped in front of the picture and Hanna asked: "Do you know Diana?"

I tilted my head and imagined the girl in platform sneakers, baggy pants and a crop top.

"That's the singer from Three for Me," I said.

Her "singing" consisted of moving her lips to the playback. Sam, her male counterpart, and the female trumpet player were also only pretenders. My father thought it would be easier technically if all the sound came from the tape. The focus was on the dance choreographies, which were to be the animation for the audience. The way the trumpeter jumped to the pounding beat, she wouldn't have had any room for real sound.

"That's right. We're in the same club as Diana," Hanna said. "I don't know how she manages to do both. I'm for stopping gymnastics practice when the music starts."

"Don't let Mommy hear that," Hilke said.

"If they don't renew her contract, we'll have to move back to where she can find a job anyway." Hanna squeezed past us and opened one of the three doors on the second floor. "And if that's in the country, she won't be able to drive us to practise every day."

"We haven't lived here long," explained Heike, who hadn't spoken yet. "Our parents split up. Everything was chaotic after that." She took the last two steps of the stairs in one go. "But we're here now."

"The only question is for how long," Hanna muttered.

We had all reached the top. After Hanna, I entered the girl's bedroom. There was a bunk bed to the right of a floor-to-ceiling window and a sofa bed to the left. The room was almost full. Makeshift closets filled the remaining space between the beds and the wall. They consisted of wooden frames with fabric stretched over them. A large Nirvana poster hung above the sofa. Instead of curtains, there were colorful bedspreads that were placed around a pole and held together with clothespins. There was a pink gym mat on the floor. The atmosphere was reminiscent of a school dormitory, it was cramped but cozy. Before I could sit down on the sofa with Hanna, I had to remove some cushions. I took the fluffiest one, a red heart with arms on it, and put it on my lap. Heike flopped down on the bed and Hilke stretched out on the floor.

"Sorry, there's not much room here," she said.

But I thought it was just right. Everything in this house seemed to have been carefully measured. Not a single square foot had been wasted. When decorating their room, the girls hadn't had to think about where to put each piece of furniture because the layout of the room only allowed for that one option.

I sank deeper into the sofa. What was it like living with sisters? Probably hiding chocolate and fighting when the other stole your favorite sweater from the clothesline. But there was always someone around and if you wanted you could sneak away unnoticed because your parents' attention was elsewhere.

"Tell me," Hanna snapped me out of my reverie. "What is it like to be on stage? Do you only perform at the weekends or sometimes also at Thursdays? Do you get the first hour off the next day?"

"Have you ever met Scooter backstage?" Hilke wanted to know. "Or Marusha?"

I looked between the sisters. How much I wished that I could have been the person that they thought I was at that very moment. They would be proud to know me and I could visit them regularly in their Lego house. They would understand that I just wanted to be normal. Their mother would teach me how to make pasta salad and we would sit in the small kitchen, laughing and talking with our mouths full. For dessert we would have that delicious cheap pudding with cream on top.

"Today isn't supposed to be about me," I said in an evasive way. "It's about your career. Ask me anything you want to know. I can explain it to you better than my dad could."

Speak their language, I heard his voice.

Yes, I would, but not in his way. Still, he couldn't blame me later.

They must have already suspected something, I would tell him. They asked me right away. What could I have done? You know I'm a bad liar. If you need someone more hardened, take Grandma with you next time.

"Is there a name yet?" asked Hanna.

"Four on the Floor," I answered truthfully.

"How cool!" Hanna clapped her hands and grabbed my shoulder. "So you're in?"

"Who else, Santa?" Hilke leaned forward, grabbed her toes and stretched. She could easily touch her knees with her nose.

The phone rang in the hall. Heike jumped up and ran out. I heard her talking softly, then she called my father. A little later he took over the conversation. Unfortunately, I couldn't understand what he was saying. But I could tell by his tone, which was grumpy at first and then became more and more unyielding, that things were going badly. A little later he came into the room and said: "We are leaving, Imelda. Ms Deringer is working an extra-shift and won't have time for me today."

He rumbled down the stairs without waiting for my

reaction, a boss used to obedience and the buzz of helpful spirits holding doors open for him and handing him his jacket. Heike did the latter. I said goodbye to her sisters and had a look at the photos again. Heike slipped a piece of paper into my hand.

"Our phone number. Your father has it too, but well..." She took a sad little pause and looked out the open door. Outside, my father was already getting into the car. "Mom has had reservations about this from the very beginning, and it looks like it's not going to work out with the dance. My parents are still fighting. Mom is worried about custody. If the social worker thinks she's letting us perform to make ends meet..." She trailed off because my father started the engine. "But I can tell you about that later. Will we meet again? That would be great."

I promised. Then I ran after the approaching car. Fortunately, my father stopped at a construction site. Maybe he didn't want to hit the concrete mixer backing out of the gate. Panting for breath, I fell into the front passenger seat.

"You think that's funny?" I shouted at him.

He slammed his palm against the steering wheel. "This sucks, this whole thing sucks."

He fished a cigarette out of the pack in the glove compartment. In a flash, I pulled out the lighter and put it out of his reach.

"Be nice and don't smoke! I'm not your employee. Or are you paying me?"

With a resigned look, he dropped the cigarette in the compartment next to the door.

"It could have been so good, Imelda." He slowed down to let a car pull out onto the road. If he was paying attention to traffic, he must be depressed. "I caught the mother at a bad moment. I should have stopped the conversation immediately and spoken to her quietly another time. Instead, I spoiled everything with my impatience. I wanted to push her to sign today. That was a mistake."

Meanwhile, he had brought the car to a stop. The horn honked behind us. My father drove up again at the speed of an elder.

"If you improve the terms of the contract, I'll try to mediate," I suggested. "Let's say you use two of the three, alternating. Then there would be only one on the bench at any given time."

"I don't know."

He turned into our street. There were old gnarly trees on both sides. I used to think they were pretty, but now even the plants in our neighborhood seemed pretentious. I really wanted to go back to the Lego house.

"I'll have a word with Fabrice," my father said. "In any case, it has to be clear: you'll do a test run first, and then we'll decide."

"Then why sign the contract now?" I wanted to know.

"To secure an option on them. To avoid that Fabrice trains them and then they go to another manager or go out on their own."

"I see."

I would have to be nicer to the triplets. My father really was a tough one. We were pulling into the garage. When he went to close the door, I asked him to leave it open.

"I am going to ride the bicycle," I said.

If he had known me any better, he would have thought that was a strange thing to do. I never did sports of my own free will. But my father just mumbled something to himself and trotted out through the connecting door and into our villa.

I pumped up the tires on my bike. I wiped the cobwebs off the handlebars and headed back. It would be easiest if the triplets were under the impression that "Four on the Floor" was about them and me. We would do rehearsals in that arrangement. I would be the lead singer and they would improvise dance moves. Soon they would have the feeling of being real artists and would be well prepared for their meeting with Fabrice. And when my father finally got to see them, he would be blown away by their concentrated power, and he would let all three of them perform. Yes, that's how it could work!

After about twice the time it had taken us by car, I arrived back at the estate.

Just before I got to the Deringer house, I was almost knocked over. Someone tore open the door of a parked car. I had to brake hard. The handlebars of my bike dug painfully into my stomach.

"Can't you watch out?" I yelled at the woman getting out of the car. "You didn't see me at all, did you?"

"Sorry! I really didn't."

She was holding the car keys in one hand and cardboard folders under her other arm. She was pale with shock. As she tried to push the car door shut with her free hand, the folders slipped out of her grasp and fell to the floor. She hastily picked them up and, after glancing at the label, threw one of them back into the car. On the passenger seat was a plastic box full of files. In the floorboard of the car I saw some snack packs and two empty beverage cartons. Maybe the lady was a sales rep for something. But I couldn't see any product samples.

"Is everything all right with you?" She eyed me with concern.

There was worry in her voice, but the way the woman seemed so upset, it wasn't just me. If I'd gotten hurt and she'd been to blame, her day would be ruined for her. She had obviously been in a hurry, hadn't even had time for a meal break, and now, in spite of her best efforts, she was causing accidents.

"I'm fine," I said. "No harm done."

"Okay." She nodded at me and then said it to herself one more time, "Okay!"

She closed her eyes for a few seconds and exhaled. Then she scurried around the car with her file, sprinted to the Deringer house, took the stairs two steps at a time, and rang the doorbell. Without knowing why, I ducked behind her car.

Through the windows I saw her being let in. Why was I hiding? I had done nothing illegal. Not yet. But I wanted to find out more about the woman, and I already suspected that this was only possible in detective mode. The hurried visitor had to be the person whose judgment Ms Deringer feared the most: the social worker. She hadn't looked mean, more like she needed help herself. She was overworked, behind on her schedule, and had too many cases. She could only attend to the most pressing matters. And that obviously included these girls. I began wondering. What could possibly be going wrong in this idyllic family home? Maybe I didn't need to speculate - the answers were right there in black and white. With a little luck, the social worker had picked up the wrong file in her haste. In any case, she had forgotten to lock the car. I leaned my bike against a tree. The car was about twenty yards from the Deringer house. From the kitchen window on the street side, I would only be visible if someone looked out at a steep angle. Just to be on the safe side, I crouched down and walked along the side of the parked cars until I got back to the social worker's car. I secured the box with the files in it and ran back, stooping low. A little further on was a small park. I sat down on a bench there and flipped through the books as if they were fashion magazines. But - by Naomi Campbell - what I read here shocked me even more than the missteps of the supermodels. If my father found out! He would be furious, devastated, helpless, but also grateful. To me, that is. I would give him the news that saved him from the biggest failure of his career.

In record time, I made my way back. I reached our villa with burning thighs and eyes watering from the wind. I found my father sitting in his study. He had drunk two cups of coffee in the hour or so I had been gone. I could tell by the rings on the mahogany top of his desk. In this household, refreshments were brought and the empty cups promptly cleared away. But none of the good spirits were to dare wipe near his piles of papers, my father was particular about that. His filing system was not to be mixed up in any way.

"Is it time for dinner?" He muttered as I entered.

"Diana has a problem," I blurted out.

"Yes, if she doesn't learn all the texts, I've been telling her for a long time." He pulled something lopsidedly copied out of a brown envelope and reached for a highlighter.

"Diana's been drugged," I said.

That got his attention.

"Certainly not, who said that?" He slammed the highlighter down on the desk. "There are no drugs backstage. And if she shares a dressing room with other performers, I'll have the makeup artists take care of her. While Diana is performing with me, she can't even get vodka."

"Maybe so," I said. "But you don't have any control over what she takes for exercise. In February, she was competing in Bordeaux, and during a routine check, something was found in her blood."

"Hormones? Steroids?"

"I don't know, it has a long name and it's banned. More importantly, they found out about her and now she's in trouble, and so are you."

"What's that gotta do with me?"

"Diana is a minor, that's why the Department of Youth Services has been alerted. Her parents are training her. So it stands to reason that they also gave her the drugs. My guess is that's-" I thought about it and searched for the term that had been used so often in the talk show of Arabella Kiesbauer: "child endangerment".

"Child shit that is!"

My father jumped up and paced behind the desk. I could literally hear it clattering around in his brain.

"The streetcar festival, when is it?" I asked.

I hadn't been very interested in this event until today, but since he kept talking about it, some details had stuck with me. The transportation company was celebrating its fiftieth anniversary with a party at the depot. "Three for Me" would be part of the show. Since there was no entrance fee, half the town and guests from out of town were expected. The prospect of so many spectators was a big deal for my father, who usually took his act only to discos.

"Saturday, two weeks from now," he groaned.

"Well, I don't know how fast the people in the department of youth services work," I said. "But if you're unlucky..."

"What would happen?" That was my father's standard phrase when my mother came to him with a problem. Many times nothing really happened, but that was because my grandparents had a lot of money to take care of problems.

"Grandma might be able to bribe the building department," I said. "But social workers have idealism. They want to help the children and save them. You're not going to get anywhere with money, on the contrary, you're just going to make yourself even more suspect. Of course the parents will try to deflect attention from themselves. They have been coaches in the club for a long time, and there have never been any problems with them. But once they allow their girl some show business, she's poisoned. And by whom?"

"Why would I put steroids in Diana's coke?"

My father stopped in front of me. I wanted to continue my thoughts, but I felt a pang of pity. We didn't get along well, my father and I, but at that moment he seemed like a boy whose favorite toy had been destroyed.

Printed in Great Britain
by Amazon